Dedication

To Granny Tricia who always believed in me. Who always told me I could be anything I wanted, the president, a doctor, a writer. I hope I have made you proud.

Patricia Ann Evans

My grandmother and best friend

1948-2005

Chapter One

November eighteenth two thousand and five probably the worst day of my life, but it didn't start off that way.

"Hey Lily," I turn around in the hall to see a gorgeous guy calling out to me. He's about six foot tall with an athletic build and a cocky grin. He has dirty blonde hair cut in a shaggy do, and the most amazing green eyes. "Hey Andy, what can I do for you?"

"Well I was wondering if you want to go out this weekend." The unbelievable just happened. The hottest guy in school just asked me out. He's completely out of my league. He's gorgeous and I'm not. I'm five foot seven, and overweight. I have dark brown hair and eyes. My best feature is my smile. So of course a stutter, "uh uh yeah I'd like that."

"Okay, I'll pick you up around six tonight. See ya then."

"Yeah, see ya." With that I head toward the parking lot and from there home.

Home was a little two bedroom house in the middle of the woods. It was my great grandparents place. I loved it. The quaint little house held the memories of a lifetime; you could feel them in every room, happiness, sadness, love. I loved the silence of the woods. It was a place where you could think. You were at a place where you could just be, with no pressure from the outside world.

"Hey Mom, I'm home," I yell as I walk in the door. My mom, Sue James, is a beautiful woman. She is five two, skinny, with graying brown hair and hazel eyes. She's tanned from years of being outside. I get my love of nature from her.

"Back here sweetie," she calls back. She sounds upset and I start to wonder what's wrong. I walk into the kitchen as she hangs up the phone. "Mom, what's wrong?"

"That was Chrissy. You know she's supposed to take granny to the doctor today. Well I need to go do that. There's something wrong."

"What do you mean there's something wrong?"

"Chrissy said she sat down on the couch and spaced out. She hasn't moved or responded to anything for a while. I've got to go."

"Okay, I'm coming with you." And with that we rushed out of the house.

We arrived at my grandmother's house in less than five minutes. I wasn't prepared for what I saw. She just sat there staring off. She didn't say anything or even look at me when a talked to her. "We're going to need help getting her into the car. Chrissy call Peter," I heard my mom say. When Peter got there he put her in the car, and my mom and I headed to Opelika to take granny to the doctor.

It took us only a few minutes to get there, but for me it seemed like forever. Momma got out and ran in to get help. They had granny in a room before I could even get out of the car. When I walked back to the room the doctor was examining her. "It appears as though your mother had a stroke. I believe the cancer spread to her brain," Dr. Brian said to my mom, "I'm sending her to Bethany House. It's a hospice center. I don't think your mother will make it through the night. I'm sorry."

I had already known my grandmother had lung cancer, but like most people I was in denial. I believed she would get better, but the whole time she was getting worse. The prognosis shouldn't have been a surprise to me, but it was, it hit me like a ton of bricks. All I could do was stand there.

My mother made all the necessary calls and then we followed the ambulance to Bethany House. The whole family showed.

Around six o'clock my phone went off, "Hello," I said in a hollow voice.

"Hey Lily, its Andy."

"Oh hey."

"I'm at your house and no one's here."

"Umm yeah, my grandmother is sick. I can't go out tonight."

"Okay, is she going to be okay?"

"Umm, yeah," I said. I couldn't manage to tell the truth.

"Okay, well I hope she gets to feeling better. Bye."

"Bye," I said and turned my phone off. I didn't want to talk to anyone. I wanted to be alone with my misery. I couldn't put on the air of being okay.

"Lily you need to go home and get some rest, Chrissy will take you," my mom said to me around midnight. "No, I left the night Paw died. I'm not doing that again. I'm stayin' with Granny. Renee brought me my medicine I'll be fine." Renee is my older sister, my only sister. She's beautiful like my mom. Renee is our mother twenty years ago.

"Lily you know you need sleep. You know you won't get any sleep here. The last thing we need is for you to have a seizure. You need to take care of yourself. There is nothing you can do for Momma."

"Mom I won't get any sleep at home and you know it, and there is something I can do for her, I can be here. I can't leave her."

"I'm not going to be able to talk you out of this?"

"No."

"Okay, just try to get some sleep."

"I will if you and Renee will."

"Okay, I'll go get your sister. Why don't you go ahead and stretch out on the couch."

Around four thirty we got up. I made it two steps before I collapsed and had a seizure. "Lily! Somebody help! She hit her head. Oh my god please let her be okay," Renee cried.

"She's going to be okay," Momma said to Renee when it was over, about half an hour later.

"Are you sure? She hit her head pretty hard," Renee replied.

"I'm sure baby. I've been through this with her several times. She just needs to take it easy. I wish she would go home."

"She won't and you know that. She's not going to leave granny. She's going to sit in that chair beside her bed until granny dies."

"I know, but this isn't good for her."

At noon on November 26, 2005, I sat by my grandmother's bed when she took her last breath. A part of me died with her. Her death was more than I could handle the fourth in less than three years. The first was my papa (my dad's dad), then paw (granny's husband), my cousin Kelly, and lastly granny the one person I could count on. It was too much in too short a period of time.

November 28, 2005, the day of granny's funeral was hell. "Hey Lily, what are you doing out here all by yourself," my uncle asked behind me. I wiped my eyes quick and turned around on the steps, "Nothing, I just needed some air. Do you need anything?"

"Just some air, Lily you know its okay to cry. It's alright to lean on someone. You don't always have to be the one everybody leans on."

"I'm fine. I'm just going to go check on momma."

"Okay," he said shaking his head, knowing he didn't get through.

We left for the funeral home about an hour later. I couldn't even walk in to the viewing room. I couldn't bear to have the picture of my grandmother in a coffin in my head for the rest of my life. Maybe I should have gone in. Maybe then I would have been able to grieve.

Chapter Two

July 24, 2006

"First day of senior year, you excited?" Mom asked as I walked in to the kitchen that morning.

"Coffee, I need coffee," I replied, "Thanks. I don't know I guess I'm excited."

"You'll probably be more excited when you wake up. Well I'll see you this afternoon, gotta go."

"Bye, love you."

"Bye, love you."

In advisement when Ms. Shenell handed me my schedule I couldn't help but wonder what the hell I'd been thinking when I signed up for classes at the end of last school year. "Hey Lily, what classes you got?" BJ asked. BJ's a sweet six foot African American. He has a great smile and an athletic build. He's the captain of the football team, and doesn't follow the rules of popularity. He talks to everyone, is nice to everyone.

"Physics, AP English, Mass Media, and Government this semester, next semester I have Calculus, Economics, Spanish, and a computer class. You?"

"Nothing that hard, Earth and Space Science, Algebra 2, Economics, and assistant, next semester English 12, Government, P.E., and assistant. Who did you get for government?"

"I lucked up Tucker. You?"

"Gowan."

"Sorry, I thought he was retiring last year?"

"He decided to stick around and torture our class instead."

"Sorry again, maybe it won't be as bad as everyone says."

"Yeah right."

"First block, Physics. Mornings are going to be just great this semester," Haley, a sweet petite brunette, said as we walked into Ms. Brant's class. "Oh yeah, why can't they at least wait till second block to schedule the hard classes? No one's awake during first," I replied.

"I know. Why did we sign up for this class anyway?"

"We didn't want to dissect anything, which eliminated anatomy, and we didn't want to be bored so bye bye to earth and space science."

"Yep, we're crazy."

"Okay everyone take a seat. I'm Ms. Brant and I will be your Physics teacher this semester. I won't tell you this class is easy because it's not, but it will be fun. We will be doing a lot of experiments and projects that you will enjoy. Okay everybody go get a book out of the closet and we'll begin."

I was the last one to get a book. That's when I found the blades. I stole one, and that's when I began cutting.

"Hey mom, can I stay at Jane's tonight," I asked my mom Friday. "Okay, I guess. Who all is going to be there?" she replied.

"I don't know. I guess the usual."

"Jace?" Jace Jacobs is my ex. I should have known better than to date a guy who looks that good. He's six two with dark brown hair and brown eyes. He has a very nice athletic build, and he cheated on me.

"I don't know. I doubt it. He has a job now. He works most weekends. Why?"

"Well I don't know probably because he's your ex."

"Operative word being ex momma."

"Okay, well go and have fun. Call if you need anything, and don't forget your medicine."

"Okay, love you."

"Love you too baby," she replied as I walked out the door.

I pulled up at Nick and Jane's a few minutes later. It's a small two bedroom house on the lake. Not the expensive side of the lake though. It's nestled between a couple of trailer parks, but it's a great place. It's always been a haven when things are going bad. It's always been the place to go when you just needed a little fun and good friends.

"Hey girl," Jace said as I walked in the door at Jane's, "I'm surprised your mom let you come with me being here."

"She doesn't know you're here."

"Of course she doesn't. She's going to hate me forever if you don't stop lying to her."

"She's going to hate you forever anyway, and if I don't lie to her you'll never see me."

"Oh well, in that case. So where's Cody this weekend?"

"I don't know. I don't really care. I don't feel like hanging out with him this weekend. How about which ever slut you're dating this week?"

"Ouch, no one for your information, I'm between sluts at the moment. That sounds like a lot more fun than what I meant."

"Ha-ha."

"Yeah I know funny. So trouble in paradise, you and Cody?"

"No I'm just not looking for a hook up tonight."

"Lily since when is a guy just a hook up to you?"

"Since I don't feel like getting serious with anyone. Look at how the last time went."

"Okay low blow, true but low blow. I thought we were past that."

"We are, sorry. Cody's just not the type I want to get serious with."

"Why not?"

"Well I can't exactly talk to him about anything. He's all about himself and what he can get out of everybody else."

"Why are you with him?"

"Fun."

"As simple as that, Lily you know you can have fun with someone you can talk to."

"No because all they ever want to do is talk," I replied with a pointed stare.

"Okay, I'll back off for now. So did you bring any money?"

"Ummm, well you see I'm kinda broke."

"Okay, I'll pay for your drinks."

"Thanks."

"But you have to promise to come to me if you need someone to talk to. Don't let it build up."

"Okay," I said grudgingly. "You know you're kinda nice for a cheating ex-boyfriend."

"Yeah I know," Jace said sadly.

"So where is everybody?"

"They went to the store to get the stuff for tonight. I told them I'd stay here and wait for you."

"Okay, but y'all didn't know that I didn't have money. So why would they leave before I got here."

"Lily, give me some credit. I knew you didn't have any money. I went ahead and gave Nick the money for yours too."

"Okay since you know me so well, what did you tell him to get me?"

"Jack."

"Okay, you do know me." The front door opened then and a tall tanned brown haired guy walked in, Jace's twin brother. "Y'all its safe they're clothed."

"Very funny Josh," I said and headed out the back door.

"Thanks a lot Josh. I'll be lucky if she says one word to me the rest of the night," Jace said angrily.

"Sorry, it was a joke."

"I know but you know Lily hates to be reminded of that. She views our relationship from last summer as a huge mistake. I really don't blame her seeing as someone told her I cheated on her, Josh."

"Sorry."

"Whatever," Jace said and headed out back. "You know smoking's bad for you."

"Yeah so what," Lily replied, "everything's bad for you these days."

"Sorry about Josh. He's an idiot."

"I know. I shouldn't let it bother me. What happened, happened we can't take it back."

"Yeah, well you want to go back in and see what games we're playing tonight?"

"Sure, who's in charge of music?" I asked as we walked back in.

"You of course, did you bring your cds?"

"Yep, just in case."

We walked back in and headed to the kitchen where everybody, Nick and Jane Abrams, and Josh, was setting up. Nick is an amazingly kind man. He stands at about five ten. He has dark blonde hair and blue eyes. In contrast his wife Jane stands at five foot, with red hair, and green eye. But though they have different physical appearances, they are both the kindest people I have ever known.

"Hey, so what are we playing tonight?" I asked.

"I was thinking quarters with rules," Josh answered.

"Fine with me," replied Nick.

"Shit, I suck at quarters. Oh well it looks like I'm getting drunk tonight," I said.

"Well you get a lot better at quarters when you get drunk," Jace said.

"True, so I won't be the only one getting drunk."

"Ummm, Lily have you taken your medicine? It's six o'clock," Jace said.

"Oh, y'all just give me a sec." I hurried into the living room to grab my medicine. When I got back everyone was sitting around the table with their drinks. "Jace, you're not drinking?" I asked when I saw the can of coke in front of him. "Nope, y'all will need a ref to play quarters with rules," he replied. I shrugged, sat down, and took a shot of Jack.

Josh went first. When the quarter rang the shot glass he just looked at me and smiled. I took another shot. He rang it two more times, making Jane and Nick drink. "Well that means I get to make a rule. Let's see, ahh I got it, no cussin', Lily will be

20

doing a shot every five seconds. Now let's see how many more times I can ring it."

"Oh Josh," I said fluttering my lashes as he made the shot and his shot went a little off. "Oh I'm sorry," I said sweetly when he gave me a go to hell look, "My turn." I missed, "Well damn it."

"Drink!" Josh yelled laughing.

About an hour later I saw Jace give Josh a not so friendly look. I decided then it was a good time for a break, "Smoke break, who's comin'?" Jane and Nick hopped up and we headed outside. "What the hell do you think you're doing? Lay off Lily. You know she doesn't need to drink a lot. She has epilepsy," Jace said as soon as he and Josh were alone.

"Sorry, I wasn't thinking," Josh replied ticked, "But the last time I checked you weren't her keeper."

"Josh if you know what's good for you, you will shut up and lay off Lily."

"Or what?"

"Or I'll kick your ass little brother. Something I should have done a year ago," Jace answered and headed outside.

"What's wrong?" I asked when Jace came out the door.

"Nothing, just brother shit."

"Okay, no fighting. I'm the only one allowed to kick y'alls asses," I said grinning.

"Too true baby," Jace said laughing.

We all went back in then. Josh was sitting at the table looking ready to commit murder. I looked back at Jace with a questioning look. He just shrugged. "Okay, let's forget about petty differences," I said looking at Josh then Jace, "and have some fun. I'm about half drunk so I should start getting better at this game. By the way why isn't there any music playing?"

"Because someone was in too big of a hurry to drink to put any on," Jace said grinning at me.

"Oh well in that case, ref I want to hear some Motley Crue," I replied.

"Okay, Motley Crue coming up for the beautiful half drunk girl."

After Jace sat back down I took my turn, and finally rang the shot glass. I looked over at Jace and grinned, "Come on big guy you have to take at least one shot tonight."

"No, I'm the ref remember."

"So, one shot won't get you drunk. Have you forgotten I've seen you drink?"

"Oh come on everyone knows he won't drink when his precious Lily is drinking," Josh piped in.

"Josh mind you on damn business," Jace replied between gritted teeth.

"Oh like you did earlier. Telling me to lay off Lily or you'll kick my ass."

"Josh I'm serious shut the hell up."

"Why? You cheated on her and now you care about her?" With that Jace leapt across the table and knocked the hell out of Josh. All I could do was sit there while Jace beat the shit out of Josh. I couldn't understand why the hell they were arguing about shit that had happened a year ago. Then I came to my senses and started helping Nick break it up.

Nick managed to get between them and push Josh up against the wall. I grabbed Jace and started pulling him toward the back door. "Hey what the hell?" I asked when we got out the door.

"He deserved it," Jace said.

"What the hell is going on? I don't get it. How the hell do I figure into one of y'alls fights?"

"It's nothing. Don't worry about it."

"It's nothing! You looked like you wanted to kill your own brother. I think I have something to worry about."

"No you don't. Trust me you don't want to know what's going on Lily," Jace said getting mad at me.

"Hey don't take that tone with me jackass. I haven't done a damn thing to you, except maybe keeping you from committing murder."

"Lily let's not get into this. Not tonight. It's not like you would believe me anyway."

"Why wouldn't I believe you?"

"Never mind," Jace said walking off into the woods.

When I came back in Nick had locked Josh in the spare room, and him and Jane were sitting in the living room. "Hey, where's Jace?" Jane asked as I walked into the room.

"Off in the woods somewhere. He got pissed off at me for asking what was goin' on. Do y'all have any idea what the hell is goin' on?" Nick and Jane shared a look that said they did, but Jane answered, "No. You know how those two are, they'll fight over any little thing."

"Are you sure?"

"I have no idea what it was about," Nick answered. I could tell they were lying to me, but I couldn't figure out why. They never lied to me.

After that Nick and Jane headed to bed, and I headed to the bathroom. I locked myself in and pulled out the blade I'd stolen from Physics class. I sat on the toilet just looking at the cuts on my arm for a minute. Then I started crying, and pulled the blade across my arm. "Why God? Why doesn't the pain just go away? Why did I have to lose the one person I could count on? Why did I have to lose all of them? Why God why? Why do I have to still love a guy who hurt me so badly? Why me?" I whispered.

I sat there for five more minutes crying. Then I got up washed my face, and went to bed. I slept on the couch that night since Josh was locked in the spare room.

An hour later Jace comes in and lies down on the floor beside me. "Hey Lily, you still up?"

"Yeah"

"I'm sorry I snapped at you. None of this is your fault."

"Why won't you tell me what's going on?"

"I will, just not tonight."

"Why not?"

"Lily trust me okay."

"Okay, but you will tell me soon."

"Yeah I will," Jace said sounding depressed.

Chapter Three

July 31, 2006

When I got out of school on Monday Cody was waiting for me in the parking lot. "Hey babe, what did you do this weekend?" he asked when I got to my car.

"Hung out with some friends, you?"

"Nothing much. Who?"

"Jace, Josh, Jane, and Nick, why does it matter?"

"I don't know I was kinda wondering why you didn't hang out with me."

"Well it's not like you were blowing up my phone."

"It's Jace isn't it? This is the second weekend in a row that you have decided to be with him instead of me."

"Oh please, me and Jace are just friends and you know that."

"Don't try that shit with me, I know better."

"Oh you do. Is that because you're constantly cheating on me? Would you like me to name them off?" Cody shoved me up against the car then and said, "You're not to see that son of a bitch again you hear me." I shoved him back and said, "No you hear me jackass, you do not own me. I will see whoever the hell I want." Cody shoved me back up against the car, and then all of a sudden he was on the ground a foot from me with Jace standing over him.

"Look you son of a bitch, you will stay the hell away from Lily. You will not talk to her, look at her, or so much as think about her," Jace said punctuating each word with a kick to Cody midsection. I just stood there looking on in amazement. Then Jace turned at looked at me, "Come on I'll drive you home."

"But my car." A '97 Chevrolet Cavalier with great gas mileage, I just wished it was a truck.

"You can get it tomorrow. I'll bring you to school in the morning."

"Umm, okay."

Jace picked up mine and his stuff and headed toward his truck, a '95 Chevrolet Z71, more my style. When we were almost to my house he looked at me and asked, "Are you okay? Did he hurt you?"

"No, I'm fine. Thanks for coming to rescue, but I was handling him."

"Damn it Lily, he could have seriously hurt you."

"No he couldn't. You know I can take care of myself."

Jace jerked the truck over to the side of the road. "What the hell are you thinking? Yeah you could have giving him a few bruises sure, but he could have put you in the hospital. Lily you are not invincible," he yelled.

"I know that," I yelled back.

"Do you really? Because sometimes I don't think you do," he said looking worried.

"I know I'm not invincible Jace. I just have to act like I am sometimes, or I'll break," I said starting to cry.

"Sweetie it's going to be okay. I won't let him hurt you. Trust me."

"I know. I do trust you," I said still crying and thinking, "it's not Cody who's breaking me, it's everything else that I can't control, that I can't get back."

The next day in Mr. Tucker's Government class, Andy leaned over and asked, "Are you okay?"

"Yeah, I'm fine. Why?"

"Well I saw the show yesterday."

"Oh that, yeah I'm fine."

"Why were you datin' that ass hole anyway?"

"I don't know."

"Lily, I know you're having a tough year, but that's no reason to sell yourself short with someone like him."

"Look Andy, thanks for the concern, but I'm fine. I thought he was a better guy than that. I was wrong, and now he's out of my life," I said a little too aggressively.

"Okay, sorry, didn't mean to tick you off."

When the bell rang I headed for the bathroom. I locked myself in a stall and pulled out my blade. A sat there looking at it for a second then I pulled it across my arm and cried. "I can't keep this up. I can't keep cutting its wrong. I have to snap out of it. There are people out there who have worse lives than me. I can handle this. I have to be able to handle this," I thought and pulled the blade across my arm again.

Wednesday was our first test in Physics. "So you ready for this test?" Haley asked as we walked into the classroom.

"Yeah, I studied a good bit last night, and we have our formula sheets. I don't think I should have too much trouble with it. How about you?"

"Yeah, I don't think this one is going to be too hard. The first test in any class is always easy."

When Ms. Brant handed out the test I realized I might have been a little over confident, but I still thought I would manage at least a B on it. I'd never made less than a B. The next day when she handed them out I realized just how wrong I had been. I had made the first F in my whole school career, and not even a high F. I made a 23. All I could do was think I can't handle this, not this. The one thing in my life that's supposed to go right, that always goes right is school. I always make good grades. What the hell are my parents going to say when they see this? If I make a B on anything I'm in trouble with them. What the hell is going to happen when they find out a made an F.? I just won't tell them. I can't tell them.

Chapter Four

November 24, 2006

"Hey girl, where have you been? I haven't seen you in a while," Jane said when I walked in one Friday afternoon.

"Just been busy with school," I replied. I must not have sounded very convincing because Jace looked up at me with a worried look.

"Well that's understandable," Jane said and walked into the kitchen.

When she was out of ear shot Jace got up and walked over to me, "Come on. I'll listen," he said. I followed him out back to the woods. "So what's going on?" he asked when we sat down under a tree.

"Nothing just been busy," I replied.

"Come on Lily," he said. He looked down and grabbed my arm, "What the hell is this Lily?"

"Nothing," I said jerking back my arm as I started to cry.

"Lily you have cuts all down your arm. Don't tell me it's nothing."

"I just... I can't...I..."

"Lily," Jace said pulling me into his arms as I started to cry harder.

A few minutes later he pulled me back and looked at me. "Baby, please talk to me," he said looking worried.

"I don't know how it started, or rather why I started. I just couldn't handle it all anymore Jace. They're all gone. They're gone and I don't know what to do without them. I don't have granny to go to when my parents are at each other's throat, or at mine. I'm failing Physics, and you know how my parents are going to react to that when they find out. It's not like I'm not trying to pass the class. I study for hours every day. I just don't get it. And everything else in my life seems to be going to hell. I keep having seizures, even though I'm taking my medicine. I had one in school the other day and..." I couldn't keep going. All I could do was sob.

Jace sat in the woods holding me for over an hour. "Come on sweetie, there is somewhere I want to take you," he said standing up.

"Where?"

"Just trust me baby, can you do that?"

"Yeah, I trust you."

He took me to the mental health clinic in town. I didn't want to get out at first. "Come on Lily. You do want to stop, right?"

"Yeah, but..."

"But nothing, this might help. Just give it a shot, for me," he said knowing that was the only way he was going to get me to go in.

"Will you go in with me?"

"Of course, whatever you want."

They took me back immediately when Jace showed them my arm. Dr. Johns was the therapist assigned to me. He's a short man, with thinning hair, and a kind smile. "Okay Miss James, the first thing I have to ask is are you suicidal?" Dr. Johns said when we all sat down in his office.

"No, I don't want to die. I'm too young to give up. I just want the pain to go away," I said vehemently, "the physical pain helps the emotional pain."

"Okay, I believe you. So what's been going on?" I told him everything. Jace sat there looking struck, looking hurt, as I told the doctor everything.

"Okay, I'm going to go ahead and tell you it will get better. You don't grieve properly. A lot of people don't. I can help you through that if you will let me. Secondly I think the reason you don't is your seizure medicine. Seizure medicine can cause some mental problems. Don't worry we can work around and through that. Thirdly, I think you should talk to you parents about the pressure they are putting on you. It's not healthy," he said when I finished.

"Okay," I said with tears still running down my face.

"How about we set you up with an appointment next week?"

"Yeah that sounds good," I said a little shell shocked all of a sudden.

"I don't know if your neurologist told you this, but with how many seizures you've been having lately you don't need to drive."

"I know. I just haven't had anyone to drive me."

"I can," Jace spoke up.

"Good, well Lily go home and get some rest. I'll see you next week."

When we got back in the truck, Jace just sat there looking out the windshield for a while. Then he said, "How could

I have not known? How could I have not seen it? I knew you were upset, but I didn't know that all of this was going on. I'm supposed to know you better than anyone, and I didn't see it."

"It's not your fault Jace. I didn't want anyone to know. You know I can hide when I want to. And I've been hiding."

"Yes but I'm supposed to know when you're hiding, and I didn't see it."

"Yes you did. You've been bugging me for months to lean on you, and I've been avoiding you because I knew you would see. You're the only one who has noticed the cuts. I don't even try to hide them. Mom hasn't even noticed them."

"But I should have noticed them sooner."

"Not long after I started cutting, I started avoiding you. I knew you would see, and I was so ashamed. I am ashamed. I told myself I would figure it out on my own. I would stop, and then I'd stop avoiding you. I told myself that you didn't need to know. That no one needed to know. It's my problem, so I'm the only one who has to deal with. Today I decided that I couldn't deal with it alone. So I came to you."

That was the first time I saw Jace cry. We sat there holding each other and crying for a while. Then we went back to Jane's.

When we pulled up at Jane's I looked over at Jace and said, "Thank you, but can you do me a favor?"

"What?"

"Will you please not tell anybody? I don't want anyone else to know."

"What about your parents?"

"I'll tell them...when I'm ready. Not today."

"Okay, I won't tell anyone, and I'll start taking you to school and home. I'll also take you to therapy."

"But you're going to a different school now. It would be out of your way to take me to school."

"So, it'll be fine. You don't need to drive. Lily just let me take care of you this little bit."

"I'm not going to be able to talk you out of this am I?"

"Nope."

"Okay, just wait till my mom leaves for work before you show up at the house."

"That's a given. I don't want to be met at the door with a shot gun."

"She wouldn't do that," I said laughing.

"Oh yes she would," Jace said grinning. "It's good to hear you laugh. I haven't heard you laugh in a while."

When we went in I called my mom, "Hey, I'm at Jane's."

"I know I got your note," Momma said.

"Yeah I hoped you would. I didn't want you to worry."

"I know. I appreciate it."

"Umm, can I stay here tonight?"

"Do you have your medicine?"

"Yes ma'am. I grabbed it went I stopped by the house. I wasn't sure how long I would be here so I went ahead and got it."

"Okay, is Jace there?"

"No, he's got to work this weekend."

"Okay, you can stay. Call me if you need anything."

"I will. Same goes. I love you mommy."

"I love you too, baby. See ya tomorrow. Bye."

"Bye."

"Why do you sound so sad when you talk to her?" Jace asked when I hung up.

"I guess because I know how disappointed she would be in me if she knew what was going on."

"Lily, she won't be disappointed in you. She'll be concerned. She loves you. She'll want to do everything she can to help."

"I know she loves me. I also know she'll be disappointed. I'm the good girl, the good daughter, the one who makes straight As and never gets in trouble. This would truly disappoint her, disillusion her."

"Okay, but I think you're wrong. You promised to tell her."

"And I will, just not today."

"Okay."

Chapter Five

November 29, 2006

I heard the horn blow as I was getting ready Wednesday morning. I ran to the door and yelled out, "Come in. I'm not quite ready yet." Jace came in and followed me to the bathroom. "Lily you're not even dressed."

"I know. I'm having a slow morning. I slept late."

"No you didn't. You never sleep late. Try that lie on someone else."

"Okay, so I'm not looking forward to school today. I just want to stay at home until time to go to the therapist. I'm nervous and a little scared. I won't be able to concentrate on school. So why should I bother going?"

"Because you might actually be able to concentrate, and maybe it'll distract you from the thought of going to see the therapist."

"I don't think so. When something is weighing on mind nothing can distract me from it."

"Okay, how about we skip today. Go do something fun. We can go down to the creek and just relax or go to Auburn or something."

"No, you need to go to school. If your mom finds out you skipped she'll have a fit."

"She doesn't have to find out. I know you're good at writing sick notes. I've seen them. I'm sure you can forge my mom's signature. You do your mom and dad's all the time."

"Well I could try. I'll have to see something she has signed, and practice."

"Don't worry I've got some school stuff in the truck she had to sign."

"Okay, the creek first, I need the quiet."

When we got to the creek, we got out of the truck I went to sit on the bank. We sat there for a long time just looking out at the water.

"So who are you seeing these days?" I asked

"A girl from school, she's not the greatest conversationalist, but she's good at other things," Jace said with a grin. I laughed and replied, "Of course she is. She's exactly your type then."

"Hey, I like a good conversation too."

"Yeah but that's what you have me for."

"True, so what about you? Are you seeing anybody?"

"No, I think that's the last thing I need. I don't think I need to add the pressure of a relationship onto all the other shit I'm going through at the moment."

"I don't know, it might be good for you. Someone to take your mind off things for a little while."

"I don't think so. Guys just want you to be happy all the time. They think you should just be happy to be with them, and that nothing else should matter. I can't pretend to be happy all the time. It's hard enough to do at home and school. If I had to do that all the time, I would truly go crazy."

"You haven't told your mom yet. You promised you would."

"I am, but not yet. When I'm doing better I'll tell her. I want to wait until she can see that I'm getting better, so she doesn't have to worry so much."

"But Lily, if you don't tell her she'll keep putting all this pressure on you to be perfect. Remember what the therapist said, it's not healthy."

"I'm handling it. I'm just ignoring it the best I can."

"You can't ignore anything. It all gets to you. It always has. I've seen it our whole lives. I've seen how hard you work to be what your parents want you to be, and I've seen how devastated you have been when you fall short. You can't keep doing it Lily."

"Don't worry so much. I'll be fine. I'm getting help thanks to you."

"Okay, I'll back off for now."

"Good, let's just sit here and listen to the quiet for a little while."

"Okay," Jace said looking worried.

Around three we left the creek and headed to the mental health clinic. When they called me back Jace got up to walk back with me. "Umm, Jace I think I should go back by myself today. Thank you but I think I need to do this myself."

"Okay, but I'm right out here if you need me."

"Okay."

I walked on back to Dr. Johns' office. "Good afternoon Miss James. How was school?" he asked when I came in.

"I skipped today. I was nervous about coming back here, and I just needed some quiet for a little while."

"Okay, that's understandable. So what did you do instead?"

"Me and Jace went to the creek, Hillabee Creek."

"Jace, he's a good friend?"

"Yeah, he's my best friend. I've known him my whole life."

"So just friends?"

"Yeah, we were together for a little while last year, but he cheated on me. I still love him, but I can't trust him."

"But you trusted him with this."

"It's different. This is different. I can trust him with this, but I can't trust him to be faithful. Can we talk about something else?"

"Sure, tell me about your grandmother."

"Granny, she was the best person I've ever known. She's the only person I knew who would always be on my side. The only person who always had my best interest at heart. Well not the only person, Paw, her husband was like that too. I guess I could talk to granny more than I could to him. They were always more of my parents than my actually parents."

"So when you lost them how did that make you feel?"

"Well when I lost paw I still had granny. It wasn't as bad with her there. I could talk to her about it and everything else. But when I lost granny I had no one. I'd lost my moral compass; I'd lost my confidant, and essentially my mom."

"That's hard. So why do you say your parents aren't much like parents?"

"They got married and had kids too young. They didn't want to stay home with me and my sister. They wanted to go out and party. They were still kids, and my dad still acts like a kid. My mom's better since granny died, but I don't know. It just seems almost like an act to me. I keep expecting her to head out to the bar every weekend."

"Do you think it's too late for her to try to be a parent? You're almost grown yourself."

"Sometimes, and sometimes I'm happy she's trying. I love both of my parents, but I'm not sure I can trust them to be there when I need them."

"Is that why you didn't go to either one of them with this?"

"Partially, I'm also expected to be perfect and the response to all of this... I wouldn't have been able to handle it."

"So you haven't told them."

"No, I'm going to tell my mom. Just not yet, I want her to see I'm getting better when I do."

"Okay, what about your dad?"

"If he never finds out it'll be too soon."

"Okay, but I really think you should tell your mom. Maybe she'll surprise you."

"Yeah that's what Jace keeps telling me. When I'm ready I'll tell her."

"I know you will. You don't seem like the type to avoid the hard things in life, at least not for long."

When my fifty minutes was up I walked back to the waiting room and Jace was still sitting there, looking down at his hands like they held all the secrets to the world. I made an appointment for the next Wednesday and we left.

"So how did it go?" Jace asked when we got in the truck.

"Good I think, or at least it's a start. I think this might really help. I threw away all my blades after the first meeting. It's a struggle not to grab something and cut when things start to get to be too much, but I promised myself I would stop."

"Good, so you want to go home or do you want to go grab something to eat? You haven't ate all day."

"Something to eat, Momma's working late so she won't know I'm missing for a while."

"Okay, food it is."

Chapter Six

December 20, 2006

My therapist appointment wasn't until four thirty that Wednesday, so Jace and I went on to my house when he picked me up from school. My mom was already home from work. It seemed like as good of a time as any to tell her what had been going. "Lily why the hell is Jace driving you around?" Momma asked when I got out of the truck. I looked back at Jace and said, "Why don't you wait in the truck for a little while. I need to talk to momma."

"Okay, I'll be right out here if you need me."

"Why don't we go in and I'll tell you everything?"

"You better have a good reason. You're grounded first of all, so he can just go ahead and leave."

"Momma let's just go in and talk please." We walked in and sat down in the living room.

"There are some things I need to tell you. Please don't interrupt. I just need to get all of this out, and if I don't do it all at once I'll never say it," I paused to see if she was going to let me talk. "Okay, you know I've been struggling with losing granny. Well things got bad. With losing so many people in a short period of time, practically failing physics, and all the seizures I've been having, I just couldn't handle it. I started cutting," I raised my sleeve and showed her the scars. She sat there shocked. I continued, "About a month ago I went to Jace. I knew I needed help. I couldn't keep cutting. He took me to the mental health clinic in town. He's been taking me to school and picking me up from school so that I don't have to drive, and he's been taking me to my therapy appointments."

"Why didn't you come to me?"

"I didn't want you to worry. You've had such a hard time with granny's death; I didn't want to add to that."

"Oh Lily, it's my job to worry about you. And what is this about you failing physics?"

"I study all the time and I just don't get it. The math part at least. I'm not actually failing the class. Ms. Brant has been putting our projects and experiments in as test so I have a B, but on all the actual test I haven't made higher than a D. The tests are nothing but calculus."

"Why didn't you tell me you were having trouble?"

"I didn't want you to be disappointed. I'm supposed to be the straight A student."

"Sweetie, all I ask is for you to do your best."

"No, you and daddy have always asked for more than that. Y'all have always expected me to be perfect, and I have news for y'all, I'm not. No one is."

"I'm sorry if we've given you the impression that we expect that. We just want you to do better than us, be better than us."

"Okay."

"So why did you ask Jace to stay?"

"I have a therapy appointment at four thirty; he's going to take me."

"Why don't you let me take you?"

"Maybe to the next one."

"Okay," she a little disappointed. "Well is it helping?"

"Yeah, actually it is. Dr. Johns, my therapist, says I'm making great progress. He thinks I can probably stop coming soon."

"That's good."

"Umm, can Jace come in? It's really cold out there."

"Yeah," Momma said looking devastated as I got up to let Jace in.

I'll let Jace in and headed to the bathroom, I heard him and Momma talking while I was gone.

"So you're seeing my daughter again," Sue said venting all her frustration onto Jace.

"Just as friends Ms. Sue."

"Yeah right, I don't believe that for a second. She's vulnerable and you decided to use that."

"Actually no, and anyway I don't think Lily is ever that vulnerable. Even at her worst Lily always uses her head and listens to her heart."

"So if you're not getting anything out of this, why are you helping her?"

"Because I've known Lily my whole life, she's my best friend, and she needed somebody."

"Why didn't you come to me when she told you?"

"Because she asked me not to, I made her promise to tell you, and I've been on her ass ever since to tell you. She's stubborn. She wanted to wait till she was better. She thought then you wouldn't worry so much. She said you'd see that she could handle it, if she waited."

"So you've been going to her therapy appointments with her?"

"I've only sat in on one, the first one. After that she told me that this was something she had to do on her on. Ms. Sue don't take this the wrong way, but lay off her. Your expectations of her are a huge part of the problem. So just lay off."

"You don't know what the hell you're talking about."

"With all due respect ma'am, I do. I've seen what y'all do to her my whole life. She finally reached the breaking point. So please for your daughter's sake back off."

When I walked back in Momma looked pissed, but she also looked hurt. "Momma, I'd like to talk some more, but we've got to get going or I'll miss my appointment."

"Okay," was all she said as Jace and I headed for the door.

When we got in the truck I turned to Jace and asked, "What the hell did you say to her?"

"The truth, and anyway where did you go? You left me in there with her alone forever."

"I heard y'all talking and thought I'd let y'all talk everything out. I guess that was a mistake."

"I don't know, maybe not. She needed to hear the truth."

"And I'm guessing you didn't sugar coat it."

"Why would I? I'm just a little pissed about the way she treats you."

"Okay, whatever, you and momma need to just stay away from each other before there is bloodshed."

A little over an hour later Dr. John was walking me out of his office. Jace got up and met us at the front desk. Dr. Johns looked at him and said, "Well, she's come along way. You should be proud."

Jace looked at me and smiled. "I am very proud of her."

"Lily, I think you can stop coming now if you want. If you don't think you're ready then make an appointment for after the first. I'll be happy to keep seeing you, but I think you can handle it on your own now."

"Thank you sir, for everything," I said smiling.

"You did all the work Lily, not me. Well, I hope y'all have a Merry Christmas and a Happy New Year, and Lily go out and have some fun." With that he walked off.

"So, are you going to make another appointment?" Jace asked.

"I think I'll play it by ear. If it starts getting hard to handle, I'll call and make an appointment. If it doesn't well then that'll be great."

"Okay, you want me to take you on home, or do you want to put off that conversation with your mom and go get something to eat?"

"A quick bite to eat then home, I'm starving, but I need to face Momma."

"Okay, let's go."

A little while later Jace dropped me off at the house. "Well here goes nothin'," I said looking toward the house.

"It's going to be fine. She's your mother, she loves you. Don't worry so much."

"Okay, see ya tomorrow."

"See ya." With that Jace turned around and left.

I walked in the house, took a deep breath, and yelled, "Momma I'm home."

"Hey, sweetie," she said coming out of the kitchen. "I made your favorite for supper, beef stew."

"Thank you, sounds great. Why don't we talk over supper?" I said. I wasn't hungry, but she had gone through a lot of trouble to fix me my favorite meal, so I was going to eat it.

"That's what I was thinking." We headed to the kitchen. We sat down at the table in silence. I didn't know where to start.

"So, how was therapy?" mom asked.

"It was good. Dr. Johns said I didn't have to come back unless I felt I needed to."

"That's good. So, Dr. Johns was a big help?"

"Yeah, he seemed to know the right questions to ask. He knew how to get to the bottom line, get to what I didn't even know was truly bothering me."

"That's good," she paused and took a deep breath, "Am I so horribly you can't talk to me?"

"No!" I said upset that I had made her feel that way. "It's not that. It's just easier to talk to a stranger."

"But you talked to Jace," she pointed out.

"Not all that much actually. He knew just enough to get me help."

"Okay, so do you want to tell me all of it?"

"Please don't take this the wrong way, but no. It's not you momma it's me. I don't want anyone to know just how weak I was."

"Okay," she said sadly.

"I promise that if I ever get like that again I will come to you. I just did want to add to your plate. You've been through so much lately. I didn't want to add more to it. You deserved a break."

"Why is it you've always cared more about everyone else, but yourself?"

"I don't know."

"Well if you want to do me a favor, you'll start taking care of yourself more, and worrying about everyone else less."

"Yes ma'am," I said smiling, "I'll try."

"Okay, now let's eat some dessert. We have ice cream."

"Sounds good. I love you momma," I said getting up to give her

a hug.

"I love you too sweetie."

Chapter Seven

So as it turns out, I didn't fail Physics. I found this out when my report card came in over Christmas break. I was very relieved; I made a B. Not my usual A but with all the hell I went through in that class I was just happy to pass. Second semester was a lot easier on me. Since I had finally gotten help with all my issues, I now knew the proper way to deal with everything.

January 26, 2007

"Hey sweetie," Andy said coming up behind me and putting his arms around me one afternoon after school. I started dating Andy at the beginning of second semester. "Hey," I said turning around to give him a kiss.

"So, you ready to go?"

"Yep."

"What did your mom say about this weekend?"

"She said since your parents would be there it was fine. I can't wait to get out of town."

"Yep, a weekend in Nashville should be awesome."

I hadn't been seeing as much of Jace as I had been though, since I got with Andy. I missed him, but I knew I had to go on with my life, and so did he. He didn't need to be constantly taking care of me. He put his life on hold to take care of me. That wasn't fair, as I told him when I started dating Andy. I told him he deserved to find that good girl who could tame his wild ways, the girl who would make him happy. He smiled sadly and said, "Okay, but I will be seeing you, right. You are my best friend after all."

"Of course, you can't get rid of me that easily."

About an hour after Andy dropped me off at home Sunday, Jace pulled up in my yard. I ran out of the house and jumped into his arms. "Well, hello stranger," he said when he set me on my feet.

"Hey, I missed you," I said.

"Well, I didn't even know you were gone," he said grinning.

"Ouch," was his response when I hit him.

"Okay, so I knew you were gone, meanie."

"So what have you been up to? I haven't seen you in a while."

"I've been seeing this girl from school. She's great, you'd like her. So, I guess everything is going good with you and Andy?"

"Yep, I had a great time this weekend. I bought you a present, come in and I'll give it to you."

He said, "Okay," and followed me into the house. "So what did you get me?" He stood shocked when I handed it to him. "You got me an autographed Hank Jr. cd. How did you manage that?"

"He was actually in the store looking at the cds they had, and when I saw I just decided to ask. He smiled and said sure no problem."

"So did you get you one too?"

"Nope, just you."

"Why?"

"Well I got to meet him, and plus I've never seen the point in getting someone's autograph, but I knew you would like."

"Thank you Lily, it's great… Oh by the way, Jane and Nick are already planning your graduation party."

"What kinda party?"

"Camping trip," he said. When I screamed yes he replied, "I take it you like the idea."

"Of course I do. I haven't been camping in a while."

"Good, because it was my idea."

"You know me too well," I said smiling.

"So, you want to go grab something to eat and tell me all about your awesome trip to Nashville?"

"Sure, just let me go ask Momma if it's okay."

"Okay, I'll head on out to the truck." I came out a minute later and hopped in the truck. "Okay let's go," I said smiling.

The next morning when Andy came to pick me up I was still half asleep. "Hey girl," he said walking into the kitchen where I was pouring myself another cup of coffee.

"Hey," I said drowsily.

"Didn't sleep well last?"

"No it's not that. I just got in late."

"I brought you home around five. I didn't know that was late."

"It's not; Jace came by after you left. We went out to eat, and lost track of time talking. It was after midnight when I got home."

"You were out till after midnight with Jace?" He asked starting to look pissed, which is something I would have noticed if I hadn't been asleep on my feet.

"Yeah."

"Lily, why the hell are you going out with him, when you're dating me?" That woke me up.

"What? What's the big deal? I went out with a friend," I said starting to get pissed myself.

"A friend my ass, he's your ex Lily. I doubt he's thinking of y'alls time together as just friends hanging out."

"Oh please, you're so off, and anyway what does it matter what he thinks. Shouldn't it matter what I think?"

"Yeah, but I'm not so sure you see it as friends either. Whatever I'm going to school, why don't you find another ride," Andy said as he stormed out of the house.

I stood there for a few minutes trying to figure out what the hell had just happened, and then I realized I needed to get to school. But my ride had just walked out my front door without a backwards glance, so I called Jace. Maybe not the smartest idea, "hey," I said when he picked up.

"Hey Lily, what's up? You never call me this early."

"Yeah well I kinda need a ride to school."

"Huh, I thought Andy had been taking you to school?"

"He has, but we just had a fight that I still don't understand, and he stormed out. So no ride."

"Okay, I'll be there in a few. You know we're both going to be late, right."

"Yeah, sorry."

"Don't worry about it. I just thought you might want to skip, seeing as we're both going to be late anyway."

"Not today bad boy. I have a test in calculus."

"Even more reason to skip."

"Not really, I just want to get the test over with."

"Okay, see ya in a few."

When Jace dropped me off at school I rushed off to my Calculus class, luckily Coach Sparks doesn't do roll call till the end of class. When I walked in Andy gave me a weird look. I went and took my seat by him and he leaned over and asked, "So who did you get to bring you?"

"Jace," I answered, and heard a stream cuss words come out of his mouth. At that moment Coach Sparks started handing out the test.

When class was over Andy jumped up and rushed out of the room. I ran to catch up with him. "What did you want me to do, stay home today?"

"No, but you could have called someone else?"

"Who?"

"Your mom," he said loud enough to cause people to look.

"She couldn't have left work," I replied.

"I don't know anyone but him."

"I called someone I knew would come. What the hell is so wrong with that? I don't get it. You have never had a problem with Jace until now."

"I know, but I'm getting tired of you always calling him when you need something, or going out with him on the spur of the moment."

"What do you want me to do check in with you before I go anywhere?"

"No, I just want you to think of me a little more, and him a little less when you need help call me instead of him."

"I'm sorry; it's just habit to call him. I've always called him. Andy he's my best friend."

"I know, but can you please try to break that habit."

"Yeah," I said as the bell rang, "I've got to go to class. Talk after school?"

"Yeah, sure," he said then we headed off in different directions.

I met Andy at his truck, a '05 Ford F150, after school. I was surprised he hadn't left me, but I was happy I'd told Jace not to come get me unless I called him back. "Good to see you didn't leave," I said when I was standing beside him.

"Yeah well, I said we'd talk," he replied.

"Come on, I know where we can go."

"Where?"

"The creek, there won't be anyone there. Well at least no one at the part I want to go to."

"Okay," he said and pulled out of the parking lot.

When we got there, I got out and headed to the bank. The last time I had been there was when Jace and I had skipped school. I pushed the thought of that day out of my head, and looked at Andy as he sat down. "This is where I come when I need to think," I said, "Not many people know that."

"Okay," he said looking confused.

"I've come here a lot since my grandmother died, but not recently. The last time I was here I came with Jace. Don't get up," I said as Andy started to do just that. "Just listen to me for a minute. Okay, can you do that?"

"Yeah, I guess."

"I went through a really hard time after my grandmother died; no one knows just how bad it was, well except for Jace. The last time I came here, we skipped school. I had my first therapist's appointment that afternoon, and I just couldn't handle school that day. So he brought me here, the place where I think the best," I paused to take a breath. "Andy, Jace was the only one who could see what was goin' on with me, and sometimes I think the only one who cared. I know you would have if I had let you know, but what you have to understand was that I didn't want anyone to know. I was so damn ashamed of how weak I was. Jace has known me my whole life, that's the only reason he could see it. The reason I call him when I need help is because I know he will come and I won't have to explain anything. It took years for that to happen. It takes time for me to trust someone that much. Damn it Andy I don't even trust my own family that much. Part of me knows I can trust you, if not I wouldn't be with you, but the other part of me that is scared of getting hurt doesn't. I know it's a lot to ask, but please just give me time."

"Okay, but will you tell me what all has been going on these last few months?"

"I'm sorry; I can't do that, not yet. My family doesn't even know."

"Then who paid for your therapy?"

"Jace."

"Oh, how can I compete with that, Lily?"

"You don't have to compete with Jace. He is just a friend."

"But it sounds more like he's the most important person in your life."

"No he's not. I'm the most important person in my life. I have to look out for myself first, and that means surrounding myself with people who care about me. If you have a problem with that I'm sorry but you'll just have to get over it. Think about this, you're one of those people, Andy."

"Okay," he said as he pulled me into his arms, "I'm sorry I've been such a jackass today."

"Yeah you have, but I'll let you off the hook this time," I said and made him laugh.

"Okay, well you ready to go home before your mom starts to worry."

"Yeah."

Chapter Eight

May 25, 2007

"Well hello beautiful," I heard from behind me, I turned to see Jace standing in the doorway of my bedroom. "I hope you don't mind, but your mom sent me on back. I guess she thought you were dressed."

"Yeah well, she knows you've seen my naked so," I replied.

"I didn't need to know that."

"Yeah, I didn't either when she told me."

"So are you excited? You graduate tonight."

"Yeah, I'm happy to be out of school, but I don't see why I have to walk," I said grabbing my dress off the bed. "Hey will you zip me up?"

"Of course, we can't have you going to your graduation in your underwear."

"So your graduation is tomorrow night, right?"

"Yep, then afterwards we're y'all headed to the creek to camp out for a few days. You still comin'?"

"Of course, did you really think I would miss a chance to go camping?"

"Naw, is Andy still comin'?"

"Yeah, how about Jenni?"

"Yep," he said with a strained look on his face.

"What's wrong?"

"Nothin'. Why?"

"I don't know, maybe the look on your face."

"It's nothin'."

"Oh I forgot your face has always been that ugly," I said to get him to laugh. It worked.

My mom came to the door at that moment, "Y'all ready to go," she asked. "Yep," Jace and I said in unison.

The next night after Jace's graduation we all, Jace, Josh, Jane, Nick, Jenni, Andy, and me, headed to the creek. I was happy to see that Josh and Jace seemed to be getting along better since that last time I saw them together. That fight had kind of worried me. Thinking of the fight I remembered that Jace had never told me what it was about. I decided to get it out of him before we left.

We all got started setting up camp when we got there. Afterwards I grabbed a beer and headed toward the bank. Andy followed me, "So I thought you said no one knew about this spot?"

"No one knows I come here to think."

"Okay, so thinking heavy thoughts?"

"Just looking forward to the summer, and hoping I like college."

"When do you leave for Troy?"

"At the end of July, you leave for Auburn at the same time, don't you?"

"Yep, sure you don't want to go to Auburn?"

"I'm sure. I'm an Auburn fan, but Troy has a better English program. We'll see each other plenty, don't worry."

"I'm not. I'll just miss you."

"I know. I'll miss you too." All of the sudden I heard somebody coming down the hill behind us. "Hey, are y'all being antisocial again?"

"Hey, Jace," Andy said.

"No, I just wanted to sit by the water. It's too hot to sit by the fire," I said.

"Too true," Jace replied. At that moment Jenni came down the hill. "I was wondering where you went," she said to Jace.

"I thought I'd come see what the two love birds were up to," he replied.

"Well, didn't you think they might want some alone time?" Jenni said sounding pissed.

"Do y'all want some alone time?" Jace asked us.

"Umm, that's wasn't actually my intention, but I think y'all might need some alone time," I said getting up and heading back to camp with Andy on my heels. We could hear them arguing all the way back to camp.

"What's your problem?" Jace demanded when they were alone.

"I don't know, maybe the fact that we haven't been here five minutes and you're already hanging all over her."

"I'm not hanging all over her. I just walked down here to see if they wanted to play quarters, but I didn't get to ask because you stormed down and showed your ass."

"Of course, put it all on me."

"Well I don't see where I did anything wrong."

"You're always talking about her, always ready to jump up and do whatever she asks of you."

"She's my friend Jenni. We've had this conversation a hundred times. The answers aren't going to change."

"Yeah well maybe that's the problem. You put her before me. I figured with Andy here you might actually leave her alone and pay attention to me."

"What do you want me to pretend they're not here? That's fucked up Jenni and you know it."

"Whatever, I need a shot. Come back or drown I don't give a damn," she said and stormed up the hill.

About twenty minutes later I looked over at Andy and he understood. "Go check on him," he said simply. I got up and headed to the bank. "Hey, you okay?" I asked when I saw Jace sitting on the bank.

"Yeah, I guess. One question, does Andy have a problem with our friendship?"

"Not anymore. I had a nice long talk with him a few months back, and now he's more understanding."

"Yeah well, I've tried talking to Jenni, but I don't seem to be getting through."

"Sorry, do you want to go back up or stay down here for the night?"

"Stay here."

"Okay, I'll go grab a cooler and our sleeping bags."

"Our sleeping bags?"

"Well, I'm not going to leave you down here by yourself. You might decide to drown yourself like Jenni recommended."

"You heard that?"

"Yep, we all did."

"Damn. Well do you think Andy will mind you staying down here?"

"Nope, because he'll probably be right beside me."

"I thought you said he was okay with our friendship?"

"He is as long as it doesn't involve sleeping in too close a proximity to each other."

"Okay," Jace said laughing.

I headed back up the hill and grabbed Andy from beside the fire. "So, how is he?" he asked when were in our tent.

"Not good he's sleeping on the bank tonight."

"So, you want to sleep down there tonight."

"Well, I figured we could."

"Oh, this is going to be such a romantic camping trip, me, you, and Jace sleeping side by side," Andy said laughing, "I'll go get his sleeping bag."

"Okay, will you grab a cooler, I think we're going to need plenty of alcohol down there," I said as Andy headed out of the tent.

"Okay." I grabbed our sleeping bags and headed back down the hill with Andy right behind me.

When we got to the bank Jace was sitting in the same place I had left him. "So she actually got you to agree to this. Wow girl, I knew you were good, but damn I think I might have underestimated you this time."

"Yeah right Jace, you never underestimate her," Andy said laughing, "anyway I knew she would bug me until I agreed so I figured I'd save time and just go ahead and agree."

"Good point; she can bug the hell out of statue."

"Hey, I'll leave both of you down here if you want to pick on me," I said while trying to hide my smile.

"No you won't. You love us," Jace said, and we all busted out laughing.

We sat around talking, joking, and drinking the rest of the night. The next morning I was woken up by someone moving beside me. Jace was getting up. "Hey handsome, what time is it?"

"Six, go back to sleep."

"No, I've got to take my medicine."

"Okay, I'm going back up to camp. I want to see if Jenni'll talk to me."

"Okay, I'll be there in a second. I'm just going to wake Andy up."

"Okay."

As Andy and I started up the hill we heard screams. We started running. When we got to camp we saw Jace holding Josh against a tree by his throat. "What the hell is wrong with you? Isn't it bad enough you screwed up one relationship for me? You had to sleep with my girlfriend." With every word Jace slammed Josh's head up against the tree. I ran forward and started pulling on Jace. "Jace they're not worth it. Let him go Jace he's not worth it." Jace finally loosened his grip and started to walk off. Josh jumped to attack when Jace turned his back, but I stepped in his way. "No the hell you don't. You son of bitch, if you go near him they'll never find all the pieces of you I spread all across this damn place." Josh stopped quick, and looked at me stricken. "Have you forgotten he cheated on you?" he asked pissed.

"No I haven't, but he's been there for me through a lot of shit, and he doesn't deserve the shit you've been doing to him."

"Ahh, now I get it. You're fucking him aren't you?" For that one I broke his nose. "Listen you son of a bitch, stay the hell away from Jace and stay the hell away from me." With that I turned around and walked off with Andy on my heels.

When we got to the bank, Andy asked, "Are you okay?"

"I don't know, I guess. Not really, I let my temper get the best of me. That's never a good thing."

"I'm sorry. I was about to step in when you broke his nose. I'm surprised he didn't hit you back."

"I'm not. He knows better than to touch me. He knows if he did even I wouldn't be able to stop Jace from killing him. No one would be able to stop Jace from killing then."

"I'm sorry; do you have any idea where Jace went?"

"Yeah, I know where he went, but let's leave him alone for a little while."

"Okay, I'll start packing up. Should I pack Jace's stuff too?"

"Yeah, the sooner he can get out of here the better. Thanks."

"For what?"

"For being so understanding and for letting me handle that myself."

"Well, I knew you could handle it, and Jace needed you. I also like to think I helped him some too."

"You did." With that Andy turned and headed back up the hill, and I headed to the fishing pond to get Jace.

"Hey," I said when I spotted him.

"Why did you step in? You could have been hurt!"

"Yeah and you could have killed your brother!"

"I wouldn't have killed him, and you know that."

"I know, but I hate when y'all fight, even if he did deserve it. Did you see me break his nose?"

"What? You broke his nose. He didn't hit you did he? I'll kill him if he did."

"No, he didn't lay a finger on me. He said a lot of shit that pissed me off, and then compounded that by saying I was fucking you. I kinda snapped."

"Wish I could've seen you break his nose," Jace said starting to laugh.

"If you had been there you wouldn't have given me the chance to."

"True, I can't believe Andy did?"

"He was standing back and letting me take care of it, until he thought I couldn't handle it on my own."

"Where's he at by the way?"

"Packing up all of our stuff, yours too."

"Oh, thanks."

"No problem, I think it's safe to say this camping trip is over."

"I guess it was a bad idea anyway."

"No, just having Josh and Jenni here was."

"Yeah, well, I think I'm going to sit out here for a little while."

"Okay, you want me to stay?"

"Naw, you and Andy can go on home. I'll call you later."

"Okay, bye," I said giving him hug.

"Bye sweetie."

May 29, 2007

I looked out my window when I heard someone pull in the yard, I was surprised to see Jace; he was supposed to be at work. I met him at the door, "Hey what's up?" I asked as he came in.

"I'm back with Jenni," he said bluntly.

"What?"

"Look she made a mistake, I get that."

"She made a mistake? She slept with your brother," I yelled getting pissed.

"It was a mistake, Lily. She was upset with me."

"I don't give a shit how upset she was with you she still had no right to sleep with your brother."

"Let's just say I can understand it," Jace said getting pissed himself.

"Oh yeah I forgot, you have experience in cheating on someone with their sibling."

"That's a cheap shot Lily."

"Well what do you expect? You come in here telling me you took the cheating bitch back, and that you understand her reasons. Damn it Jace, she didn't even have anything to be upset about."

"Oh really, you don't think how much time we spend together should upset her."

"No, I don't. We're just friends."

"I seem to remember not too long ago Andy had a problem with it."

"Yes, and I explained to him how much your friendship means to me."

"Yeah our friendship," Jace said sarcastically.

"What do you mean by that?"

"I don't think we should be friends anymore. I'm tired of always saving you."

"What the hell? I seem to remember it the exact opposite this weekend."

"You should've just stayed out of it."

"Well I figured a friend would step in and defend another friend," I yelled, "oh, but you don't want me as a friend."

"No, I don't," Jace said calmly, "bye Lily." He turned and walked out.

Jace made it a mile down the road before he pulled over. "I did the right thing," he said to no one. "I can't keep this up. I can't keep just being her friend. She'll never take me back. She believes I cheated on her. If she can believe that then she doesn't really trust me. Damn it," he said hitting the wheel as he started to cry.

Back at the house, I crumpled into a heap on the floor crying. "What the hell just happened?" I said to no one. A little while later the front door opened, I looked up expecting Jace. It was Andy. I started crying harder. "What's wrong?" Andy asked rushing over.

"Jace, he...we...we had an argument, and he said we shouldn't be friends anymore," I said as I rocked in a ball.

"Oh sweetie, I'm sorry. What was the argument about?"

"He's back with Jenni. I told him he was crazy. She didn't deserve another chance, and he went off."

"Oh sweetie, he'll come around. Y'alls friendship has lasted through a lot worse."

"I don't know, Andy. This time was different. He didn't have that look today when he left."

"What look?"

"The look of regret, the look that says he regrets what he just said. He walked in with that look, Andy. And when he left it was gone."

"I'm sorry. What can I do?"

"Just hold me, please, just hold me."

Around one Andy left to run some errands. What I didn't know was those errands included a confrontation with Jace. Jace had lined up a construction job for after he graduated. Andy pulled up at the construction site, and stormed out of the truck. He headed right for Jace. "What the hell we're you thinking?" he yelled.

"I was thinking Lily has you now and doesn't need me anymore."

"If you really think that you don't know her as well as you thought. I found her curled in a ball on her living room floor, for god's sake."

"She'll get over it. I don't need her shit anymore. I'm tired of always having to save her."

"Really, I haven't seen you saving her recently. Lily's been doin' a damn good job of taking care of herself recently."

"Yeah well, if it wasn't for her me and Jenni wouldn't have had any problems."

"Do you really believe that?"

"Yeah, I don't need this shit anymore."

"Fine, stay away from her."

"That was the whole point."

"No, I mean stay away from her forever. In a few weeks you'll start to regret this, but don't go to her looking for forgiveness. If you do I'll beat your ass."

"Whatever." With that Andy left.

While Andy and Jace were having it out, my mom came home. "Hey," she said walking into the kitchen. Then she saw my face, "Baby what's wrong? And don't say nothin', you've been cryin'."

"Me and Jace had an argument."

"Y'all will work it out."

"I don't think so."

"Just go talk to him."

"I don't think that's such a good idea."

"Why?"

"He said he didn't want to be friends anymore."

"Well then, he can just go to hell."

"Mom," I said laughing.

"Well, he's the one who's losing someone great in his life."

"Thanks mom. I love you."

"I love you too. How about we go out and have some fun tonight?"

"Sounds great."

"Olive Garden and Books-a-Million."

"Perfect. Thanks," I said giving her a hug.

Chapter Nine

July 28, 2007

    The day I left for Troy was bitter sweet. I was so excited about going off to college, but I was already starting to miss everyone. I kept expecting Jace to pull up and wish me luck before I headed out. "Hey, whatcha doin' out her all alone?" Andy asked walking out to stand beside me on the porch.

"Just thinking," I replied.

"Thinking about what?"

"How much I'm going to miss everyone."

"You'll see us all the time. You're not moving that far away, it's about a two hour drive."

"Yeah, I know it just seems farther than that," I said thinking of Jace.

"I'm sorry he didn't show."

"Who?"

"Jace."

"Oh."

"It'll be okay. I promise. He'll come around eventually, and if he doesn't his loss. He doesn't deserve a good friend like you."

"Thanks," I said smiling, "So are you going to stay with me my first night in my new apartment?"

"Of course, but don't say that too loud. I don't want your momma to point that rifle in my face."

"She wouldn't do that," I said laughing.

"Yeah right, I don't believe you."

"Well she's a little protective."

"A little my ass, do you remember what she said to me when I came to pick you up for our first date?"

"That if you tried anything no one would ever find the body. I laughed for weeks at the look on your face when she said it."

"Well she did scare me to death."

"Yeah, and you kept coming around. That made me like you even more."

"Yeah well I thought you were worth it."

"I love you," I said looking into his beautiful green eyes.

"I love you too," he said and kissed me tenderly.

Momma and Andy helped me move into my new apartment that afternoon. "So what do you think?" I asked when we had brought the last box in.

"Well, it's not extravagant," Andy said.

"What he's trying to say nicely is it's a dump, but we'll take care of that," Momma said, "When we get everything unpacked and put up it'll look a lot better." It truly was a dump. A one bedroom apartment that looked like it had barely survived a hurricane which is why I got it for so cheap.

"Thanks mom. It really does look like a dump," I said laughing.

"Does the plumbing even work?" Andy asked.

"Of course, do you think I would rent anything with faulty plumbing? You forget my dad's a plumber."

"Speaking of your dad, when do I get to meet Mr. Albert James?"

"Whenever he decides he wants to see me. He didn't even show up at graduation."

"Sorry," Andy said.

"Don't worry about him Lily. He'll come around. He always does," Momma said patting me on the back.

"What happened? Why did he stop coming around?" Andy asked.

"I don't know. He just does that every so often," I replied, "well, we better get started. These boxes aren't going to unpack themselves."

Around six Momma left to go home, I told her Andy was going to stay a little longer to help me finish putting stuff up. She gave me the look that said I'm not an idiot. "Well, I guess this is bye for now. My baby is all grown up. I love you sweetie. Keep your doors locked," she said when I walked her to her car.

"Yes ma'am. I love you too. Call when you get home."

"Of course, love you baby."

"Love you too mommy."

Andy joined me in the parking lot as I watched her tail lights disappear. "You goin' to be okay?" he asked as we stood there. "Yeah, I'm just going to miss seeing her all the time. Part of growing up, right?"

"Yeah, but it'll get easier."

"I know. Thanks. So, let's get finished so we can relax," I said with a grin.

"Relax huh, what did you have in mind for relaxation?"

"Umm, I guess you'll just have to wait and find out."

"Oh so not fair."

"Life's not fair."

"Tease."

"Never said I wasn't," I said laughing as he threw me over his shoulder.

The next morning I woke up to the smell of coffee. "Hey," I said walking into the kitchen.

"Good morning sleeping beauty," Andy said giving me a kiss.

"What are you doing up so early? I'm the early riser in this relationship."

"Couldn't sleep, I had this really hot naked woman asleep beside me."

"Uh-huh, can I have some of that coffee or are you going to keep torturing me with the smell?"

"One coffee coming up."

I took a sip when he handed me the cup, and sighed in bliss. "If I'd known coffee would make you sigh like that I would have been pouring coffee into you since we first started dating. I don't think I even heard that sigh last night."

"You didn't that's sigh is specifically for coffee. So, what time do you have to leave?"

"Around noon, my parents are meeting me in Auburn to help me unpack."

"Okay, so what do you want to do until then?"

"Well, I've had this particular image in my head since I woke up this morning."

"And what's that," I said grinning.

"Oh, I think you know. It involves you with a little less clothing on," he said looking at my tee shirt, "By the way, what's under that?"

"Why don't you come and find out?"

After Andy left I was at a loss for what to do. School wasn't starting until another week. I didn't need groceries; we'd taken care of that the day before. The bookstore wouldn't be open until the next day. I tried to read for a little while, but I kept thinking of Jace. Wishing I could have seen him before I left. So I decided to call him, and Jenni answered his phone.

"Hello," I heard a female say.

"Umm, hi is Jace there."

"Who is this?"

"Lily."

"Look bitch he told you to leave him alone. Why don't you just do what he says and stay out of our lives? You've caused enough trouble." Then I heard the dial tone.

While I sat there in shock, Jace walked out of a bathroom miles away. "Who was that?" he asked.

"Just your little bitch."

"What?"

"Lily, I thought you said that was over."

"There was nothing ever goin' on. What did she say?"

"Nothin', I didn't give her chance. It doesn't matter anyway. All she does is cause trouble."

"Damn it Jenni, what if she's in trouble?"

"Oh come on, she's never in trouble. She just likes to cause problems. You don't need her anyway, you have me."

"Damn it Jenni, you don't know her. Why don't you grow up?"

"Why don't you grow up and realize you're better off without her in your life?"

"Yeah sure, I'm better off. I've been miserable for the last few months, but you don't give a shit. You're perfectly fine with that because you got what you wanted. Damn it Jenni, I gave up my best friend for you."

"Your best friend huh, well I believe you get more from me than you have ever gotten from her. She's not worth losing me over, or have you forgotten the reason you dropped the bitch in the first place because you lost me."

"Fine, whatever Jenni."

"So you see it my way?"

"Sure why not?" Jace said. It's not like I can get what I truly want anyway, he thought. "Well, I've got to get back to work. I'll see you this evening. I love you."

"Love you too. Forget about her," Jenni said as Jace walked out the door.

Chapter Ten

August 3, 2007

My eighteenth birthday, the day I had been looking forward to for years. Finally an adult, but it was bitter sweet. This would be my first birthday without Jace. I'd finally realized that Jace was out of my life for good, with a little help from Jenni.

"Hey beautiful, you ready for your big birthday weekend?" Andy asked walking in the front door.

"Yep, I've been all packed up for days," I replied.

"So, how was your first week of school?"

"Great, I'm actually enjoying my classes. How about you?"

"Well I don't know if I can say I'm enjoying all of my classes, but so far so good."

"I'm glad. Let's go; I can't wait to get to the creek."

As Andy and I set out for Jackson's Gap, Jace sat at Jane's. "So, how have you been?" Nick asked coming into the living room with two beers.

"Good, everything between me and Jenni has been going great, and work's been going good."

"Good to hear."

"Yeah."

"So why do you look so sad?"

"Today's Lily's birthday. We would usually be headed to the creek right now."

"Yeah, I know. Me and Jane are meeting her and Andy down there in a couple of hours."

"Oh, I didn't know y'all were going to go camping this year."

"It's a tradition."

"Yeah, I went down there this morning before I went to work."

"Why?"

"I just had to go there today. It's her birthday. It felt too wrong not to go, even if it was just for a few minutes."

"Why don't you just talk to her?"

"Because if I do I'll lose Jenni, and anyway I doubt she wants to talk to me."

"Oh come on its Lily, and anyway you know Jenni's not the one for you."

"But the one is with someone else, and he's a great guy. He's good for her."

"You know if you had told her that Josh lied she would still be with you."

"Actually I don't know that. She believed him, Nick. She trusted Josh more than she did me."

"Well if you had told her the reason he lied, maybe she would have believed you."

"No she wouldn't. She didn't see it, just like I didn't see it until it was too late."

"Well I still think you should talk to her, but it's your life, your choice."

"Yeah, well I guess I'll see y'all later. Tell Jane I'm sorry I missed her. I'll come by next week."

"Okay, see ya later."

While Andy and I were fighting Montgomery traffic, Jane and Nick were discussing Jace and me. "Hey," Jane said coming in the front door.

"Hey, Jace came by. You know he is the biggest idiot in the world."

"Yeah, what did he do this time?"

"Lily."

"He did Lily," Jane said raising her eyebrow.

"You know what I mean. He misses her like crazy, but he won't talk to her."

"Still?"

"Nope, he came by here because it's her birthday and he was depressed, not like he would ever admit that."

"True, so what did he say?"

"That if he talked to Lily Jenni would leave him. I pointed out that Jenni wasn't the one for him, and he said he couldn't have the one for him."

"That's bullshit; all he has to do is tell her the truth."

"But he won't, he doesn't think she will believe him. He said she trusted Josh more than she did him then, and he doesn't think that has changed."

"Yep, idiot, how long do you think he will keep this up? It's been two years."

"I don't know, but I don't think he'll be telling her the truth anytime soon."

We arrived at the creek around six; Nick and Jane were already there. "Hey guys," Jane said as we got out of the truck. "Hey," I said as I walked over to her and gave her a hug.

"Happy birthday, my little girl is all grown up," Jane said smiling at me.

"That's what my mom said when we stopped by to see her. I tried to talk her into coming, but she said she gave up camping years ago. She likes the comforts of a house. She said we would celebrate tomorrow night."

"How's she doin'?"

As Jane and I discussed my mom, Andy walked over to Nick to ask a specific question. "Is he coming?" he asked when he was standing beside Nick.

"No, he stopped by the house today. He refuses to even talk to her. He's miserable, but he thinks staying with Jenni is worth it."

"Why do I get a feeling there is more goin' on than that argument?"

"Because there is, but it's not my place to tell you. And Lily doesn't know."

"Well he should tell her. She's living her life, but I see that look in her eye every now and then the look that says very loudly that she misses her best friend."

"Yeah, Jace has that look too. I don't know if he'll ever tell her the truth, but I wish he would."

"Yeah me too," Andy said. Nick looked out over the creek and thought no you don't because when he does Lily's going to break your heart, and I'm truly sorry for that.

That night was the most fun I'd had in a long time. Good friends, good drinks, and just overall good fun. It was just what I needed. I hardly even thought of Jace, and when I did I wasn't quite so sad, I was pissed.

We left the creek around noon the next day. "So, was this better than the last camping trip?" Andy asked on our way home.

"Duh, last time Jenni and Jace got in an argument, Jenni decided to sleep with Josh, Jace tried to kill Josh, I broke Josh's nose, and in the end Jace decided it was all my fault and that he didn't want to be my friend anymore. Yeah, I say this was way better."

"True, but did you have fun, really?"

"Yeah, I haven't had that much fun in forever."

"Oh so every weekend when I come to see you, you don't have fun?"

"Of course I do, but we never leave the apartment."

"Whose fault is that? You always look so damn sexy. I can't help myself."

"Ha-ha, well that's fine with me."

"I thought so," he said grinning.

"I think you're startin' to get a little too cocky."

"I thought you liked cocky."

"Okay, stop being perverted. You know what I mean," I said laughing.

"So, what are you and your mom doing tonight?"

"The usual, dinner out and Book-a-Million."

"You have a birthday ritual with everyone."

"Not everyone," I said sadly.

"Still haven't heard from your dad?"

"Nope, not since he called to tell me he was going to Florida for work."

"What? That was Monday right?"

"Yeah."

"Didn't he wish you a happy birthday then?"

"Nope, I think he forgot."

"I'm sorry," he said leaning over to give me a kiss on the cheek.

Andy dropped me off at my mom's and headed home to see his family. I walked in and saw a huge banner over the kitchen door, "HAPPY BIRTHDAY." "Mom," I yelled out laughing. She came in to the living room, "So you like?"

"You didn't have to do that."

"I know, but you're a grown woman now. I felt like giving you at least on big gesture."

"Thanks mom."

"So did you have fun last night?"

"Yeah, I think it's just what I needed."

"Good, I hope tonight will be too."

"Dinner and books?"

"Yep."

"That always makes me happy."

"Good, well come on into the kitchen. I've got you another surprise." I followed her into the kitchen and saw my sister, Renee, icing a cake.

"Oh my god, when did you get here?" I yelled running over to give her a hug. Renee moved to Georgia after our grandmother died.

"Last night, I couldn't miss my little sister's eighteenth birthday," she said smiling.

"Is that my cake your icing?"

"Nope, mine;" she said sarcastically, "of course it's yours. It is your birthday."

"What kind of cake?"

"Chocolate and strawberry."

"Oh, I love you, please tell me you're almost finished and there's coffee."

"Okay, you can have cake before dinner, I guess," my mom said from behind me, "seeing as it is your birthday."

"Thank you," I said pulling them both into a hug, "I thought last night was just what I needed, but this is better. I love y'all."

"Love you too," they said in unison.

"Well go take a shower; you look like you slept outside last night. Oh wait you did," Renee said grinning, "I'll never understand why people like camping."

"That's because you're a girly girl. Something I've never been," I replied, and headed toward the bathroom.

We ended up eating at Olive Garden that evening. "So, what did Andy give you for your birthday?" Renee asked after we'd ordered.

"Money, he told me to go buy as many books as I could. He didn't know what to get me," I replied.

"Well, that I get. The only thing I can ever think of is books, and I have no clue what books to buy you," Renee said.

"Yep," my mom agreed, "That's why I always take you to Books-a-Million. I let you pick out what you want."

"I'd be happy with just a Happy Birthday," I said.

"We know, but we want to give you more," Momma said smiling.

"Well thanks y'all," I said. I was just happy to be hanging out with my mom and sister.

Chapter Eleven

December 15, 2007

Exam time, the worst time of year for any student, and I was no different. It was eleven o'clock that Saturday night when I called Andy. "Hey baby," he said when he answered.

"Hey, whatcha doin'?"

"Studyin'. You?"

"Sorry I didn't mean to interrupt."

"It's okay. What's up?"

"I'm stressed out about these damn exams."

"Why? I've never seen you stressed about exams before."

"Yeah, well in high school I'd call Jace and we would go to the creek, fish or just sit around talkin' until I forgot to be stressed about them."

"Oh, so you need a distraction. Umm let's see what can we talk about to distract you? I have an idea."

"Oh you do? Don't you need to be here for that?"

"Well that would be more preferable, but I think we can manage some fun over the phone," he replied as I laughed.

December 21, 2007

I was still packing when Andy showed up to take me home for Christmas break. "Come in," I yelled when he knocked.

"You should look to see who it is before you yell come in," he said walking into my bedroom and giving me a kiss.

"I knew it was you."

"And how is that?"

"I knew what time you would get here."

"That still doesn't mean you knew it was me."

"Okay, so I'm psychic."

"Uh-huh," he said looking down at my suitcase, "You're not packed yet?"

"No, I've been studying like crazy all week, and I just got finished with my last exam."

"Okay, you want some help?"

"Yes, please."

"Okay, what do you want me to grab?"

"All the winter clothes out of the closet."

"Why? You won't be gone that long and I know your mom owns a washing machine."

"Yes, but I don't know what I'm going to want to wear while I'm there."

"Women," Andy said shaking his head. "So, how do you think you did on your exams?"

"Good, actually," I said smiling.

"So all that worry and stress was for nothing."

"No, all that worry and stress made me study like a fiend which is why I did so good on my exams."

"Have you already gotten your grades?"

"No, but I have a good feeling about them."

"Well good."

"So, how about you?"

"I'm not as confident as you, but of course I never am."

"True, I'm sure you did great. You always do."

"Thanks, so are you ready now. I think you have half of your apartment packed."

"Not half," I said smiling and shaking my head, "and yes I'm ready. I can't wait to see everyone. I love the holidays. It's one of the few times a year I get to see my dad."

"So he's coming home for Christmas?"

"Yep, or at least that's what he told my grandmother."

"Well good, I can't wait to meet him."

"Glad to hear you say that but do me a favor."

"Anything."

"Don't jump his ass about him not coming around me a lot. It'll just make things worse."

"Okay, but why would you say it would make things worse?"

"Jace did once. At first I was fine with it. Someone had finally said to Daddy what I had been wanting to say for years."

"Then?"

"Then Daddy didn't talk to me for almost a whole year."

"Ouch."

"Since then, everyone just keeps their mouths shut about it."

"Well I won't say a word, but what would make you think that I would anyway?"

"Because he's goin' to grill you like an over protective father, that's what set Jace off. Daddy started grillin' him, and Jace just told him he didn't see where it was any of his damn business seeing as most of the time he acted like I didn't exist."

"Damn, so your dad didn't take the truth very well?"

"To say the least."

"Well don't worry; I'll bite my tongue no matter what he says."

December 25, 2007

Momma, Renee, and I left the house headed to Granny and Papa's house around eight o'clock Christmas morning. Ever since Granny Tricia had died Momma had been going with us to Daddy's momma's house for the holidays, even though they had been divorced for years. Andy pulled in behind us as we were getting out of the car. "Hey, you look good, but we don't usual get all dressed up. Didn't I tell you that?" I said when he walked over to help us get stuff out of the car.

"Yeah, but I figured it would make a good impression," he said leaning down to pick up presents out of the trunk. "Do I have a present in here?"

"Maybe, did you bring me one?"

"Maybe."

When we walked in I saw Andy's jaw drop. It was a mad house, just like every year. There were kids running around everywhere. People crowded in the kitchen cooking or swiping food. "Umm, how am I supposed to remember all their names?" he asked looking worried.

"Don't worry no one expects you to," I said trying not to laugh.

"Why didn't you warn me?"

"Well, I figured you'd run for the hills if I did, and plus I would have missed this look on your face," I said taking a picture.

"Hey, not fair," he said grabbing a camera and taking a picture of me.

My dad chose that moment to introduce himself. My dad is a very intimidating man, just his looks usually scare people, but I've always thought of him as my big teddy bear. He's five eleven and stocky. He has graying brown and a permanent scowl, which makes it so much more special when he does smile. "Hello, I'm her dad. Who are you?" Daddy asked in a not so nice tone.

"Andy Jones sir, nice to meet you," Andy said holding out his hand to shake my dad's. Daddy just looked at his hand. Then he looked back up at him and said, "Let me guess a suck up, even worse than the last Lily. At least he had a spine even if he was a worthless jackass."

"Good to see you Daddy," I said giving him a hug. "I need to take this stuff into the dining room. Andy you want to help me?"

"No, he can stay here and talk to me," my dad interjected before Andy could answer.

By the time we sat down to eat at ten Andy looked ready to commit murder. "I'm sorry," I whispered in his ear.

"How much longer do I have to play nice?" he replied through gritted teeth.

"About an hour or so, we still have to open presents."

"Okay, I think I can make it an hour. Then we're going to my parent's, right?"

"Yep."

"Good, at least he's being nice to you," Andy said sighing.

"Yeah, he usually is when I see him."

"Well, I can bite my tongue then."

"Good, thank you. I know this isn't easy."

"I can do it for you," he whispered smiling at me.

After everyone had had their fill of Christmas dinner, we all went to the living room to open presents. I was shocked when I opened Andy's. "What? It's beautiful. It's too expensive," I said looking at the cameo in the jewelry box.

"No it's not too expensive," Andy said smiling. "You want to put it on?"

"Of course." After he helped me put it on I leaned over and said, "Thank you. I love you," and gave him a big kiss.

"The only problem is my present is going to fall short," I said handing it to him. He opened the bag and pulled out the hat I'd bought him. "Auburn hat, perfect," he said smiling, "thank you."

We left not long after that and went to his parent's. Their house was nowhere near as crazy as Granny's. When we walked in everyone was sitting in the living room watching "A Miracle on 34th Street". "Well, little brother finally made it," Andy's brother, Jacob, said smiling as we came in. "Hey Lily, are you keeping this jerk in line?" he asked as he gave me a hug. If I wasn't with Andy, I'd probably go after Jacob. He's sweet and charming, and he doesn't look half bad. He's tall and athletic like Andy, but instead of blonde hair he has dark brown hair.

"Tryin'," I answered laughing, "It's good to see you. I haven't seen you since graduation."

"Yeah, well the Army keeps me busy."

"Good to see you Jacob," Andy said giving his brother a hug before he headed over to talk to his mom. Mrs. Jones is what everyone thinks of when they think of the perfect mom. She's beautiful in a subdued way. Andy gets his blond hair from her, though it is a little hard to tell seeing as most of hers is gray now.

"Hey mom," he said giving her a hug.

"Merry Christmas," Mrs. Jones answered. "And the same to you Lily," she said when I walked over.

"Merry Christmas Mrs. Jones," I said giving her a hug.

"Did y'all save any room to eat some of this wonderful food your mother has cooked," Mr. Jones asked. Andy and Jacob get their build from their dad. He's tall and athletic. Jacob has his hair. I look at Mr. Jones and see Jacob in twenty years.

"Some," Andy said, "Merry Christmas Dad."

"So how was your first Christmas dinner with Lily's family?" Jacob asked as we sat down.

"Umm, good," Andy answered.

"Good huh, then why do you look like you just swallowed a lemon," Jacob retorted laughing.

"My dad gave him a hard time," I replied.

"Is that all?" Jacob asked laughing.

"That and I didn't quite prepare him for how many people would be there."

"And why didn't you?" Mr. Jones asked smiling.

"Give me my camera, Andy," I said. "I'll show you," I said when he handed it to me, and I showed them the picture I took when we'd walked into Granny's.

"Okay, I see why," Mr. Jones said laughing along with everybody else.

"Okay, enough laughing at my expense," Andy said laughing along with us.

After that I went to help Mrs. Jones finish dinner, and Andy stayed in the living room talking to his dad and brother. "So how much of a hard time did her dad give you?" Jacob asked.

"Let's just say it took all I had not to deck him," Andy answered.

"That bad?" Mr. Jones asked.

"Yeah, he doesn't talk to her for most of the year. Doesn't know anything that is going on in her life, and thinks he has the right to be the over protective, judgmental father. Well, at least she warned me about him."

"So did you go off on him?" Jacob asked expectantly.

"No, Lily asked me not to before I even met him. The last time someone did that he didn't talk to her for a year. I mean not at all, not one word, for a year."

"Damn, he sounds like a jackass," Jacob said.

"Yeah he is, but he's Lily's dad and she loves him."

"Doesn't it bother her that he acts like that?" Mr. Jones asked.

"Yeah, but she just shrugs it off the best she can. She's used to it. She says he's been like this as long as she can remember."

"Poor girl," Mr. Jones said.

"Yeah, but she's strong. She bounces back from everything. She's the most amazing person I've ever met."

"You're in love with her, aren't you?" Jacob asked smiling.

"Yeah, I am."

"Don't tell me her Christmas gift is an engagement ring?" Jacob teased.

"No, it's not. We're still in college, at two different colleges. It's too soon to think about that."

January 5, 2008

I was woken up a five thirty in the morning by someone holding a cup of coffee under my nose. "Huh, coffee," I mumbled. Andy laughed, "I knew that was the best way to wake you up." I opened my eyes to see my very handsome boyfriend sitting on the edge of my bed holding two mugs of coffee.

"Coffee," I repeated grabbing for a mug.

"Okay, I'll give it to you," he said laughing. "It's good to see where I fall on your list of priorities."

"How did you get in?" I asked when my brain started to work.

"Your mom lent me key."

"What? Why would she do that?"

"Because she knew I wanted to surprise you."

"Huh, surprise me?"

"Do you know what today is?"

"Umm..."

"Our one year anniversary."

"Oh, sorry I'm not good at keeping up with things like that."

"Obviously not. Good thing I am. I have the whole day planned. Well actually the whole weekend. Get up and pack a bag."

"Huh, where are we going?"

"That's a surprise. Pack enough for a couple of days, and casual clothes will be fine."

"Okay, but where are we goin'?"

"Not tellin', hurry up time's a wastin'," he said and headed out of the room.

I sat in bed a minute drinking my coffee, trying to figure out where he was taking me. In the end I got up took a shower, got dressed, and packed. "Okay, I'm ready, but there better be more coffee at this ungodly hour," I said walking into the kitchen where Andy was sitting drinking another cup of coffee.

"There is. I've already filled a thermos up," he said grinning.

"Okay, what about breakfast?"

"Doughnuts in the car, chocolate doughnuts."

"Okay, you've convinced me. I'll go anywhere with you for coffee and chocolate doughnuts," I said laughing.

When we got in the truck, I looked over at him and smiled sweetly, "So, baby where are we going?" I asked again in a sugary voice.

"You'll find out soon enough."

"Oh come on."

"You'll find out soon enough. Just sit back drink your coffee, eat a doughnut, and enjoy the ride," he said laughing.

When he turned onto 280 headed toward Birmingham, I yelled, "Tennessee. I'm right, aren't I?"

"Ding, ding, ding."

"Okay, but what part of Tennessee?"

"You'll find out soon enough."

"Damn it I'm starting to hate those words," I said pretending to be mad.

About five hours later we arrived in Nashville. "Well do you like your surprise so far?"

"Yeah, thank you," I said grinning.

"Good, I thought you might. You had so much fun when we came last year with my family, I thought it would be a good anniversary present."

"Thank you," I said again leaning over to give him a kiss on the cheek.

When we got to the hotel I was shocked, "Andy, do you have the money to spend on this place?" I asked. It was one of those huge hotels that celebrities stay at. The type of place that doesn't have rooms, but suites, defiantly not something I was used to.

"Don't worry about it," he said grinning, "why are you always so worried I'm spending too much money?"

"Because I'm not used to it, my family doesn't have a lot of money. I'm more used to counting pennies."

"Okay, but at least for this weekend forget about how much things cost. Trust me I can afford it. I have a trust fund remember."

"Yeah don't remind me. I sold out," I said sarcastically making him laugh.

"Come on let's get checked in."

After we were settled in the hotel we headed out to get lunch. The restaurant we went to was just a little whole in the wall dinner. I thought it was perfect. "I'm surprised you didn't want to go to some fancy restaurant," I said looking around smiling.

"Fancy restaurants aren't your style. I knew you would like this place. I here they have the best pecan pie."

"Well I'm not so sure about that, I make the best pecan pie."

"I can agree with you on that one. Seeing as I finally got to taste your pecan pie not too long ago."

"So, I'm starvin'. Hand me a menu." I ordered the country fried steak plate, Andy got a hamburger, and we shared a piece of their famous pecan pie.

About an hour later we headed out, "So what do you want to do now?" Andy asked when we were standing on the sidewalk.

"Just walk around. I like hearing all the street musicians. There is a ton of great artist around here, you hear them everywhere."

"Okay, a nice long walk then."

When we got back to the hotel he surprised me with tickets to the Grand Ole Opry. "Wow, can this weekend get any better?" I asked smiling.

"I thought you might like it," he said grinning pleased.

"Well, we might want to get ready? We don't want to be late. I didn't think we would be out as long as we were."

"Well if you had told me before we could have come back to the hotel early," I said smiling.

"Yeah but that wouldn't have been as much fun, and you were enjoying walking around Nashville."

"True, I'll hurry."

"We can save time if you'll let me shower with you."

"That want save time and you know it."

"Well I think we have a little extra time," he said grinning.

"Okay," I said running off to the bathroom leaving a trail of clothes behind me.

Later on that night I was in heaven when George Strait came on stage at the opry. "Oh yes," I whispered happily.

"Yeah, I thought you would like tonight's line up. I know you love George Strait."

"Thank you, I love you," I said leaning over and giving him a kiss.

When we left the opry that night I was in a euphoric mood. "God, this is the best weekend," I said smiling.

"I'm glad."

"You're having fun too, right? I don't want this to be all about me."

"I'm having fun too. I love country music. I love Nashville. And most of all I love you," he said leaning down to give me a kiss.

The next morning we headed back to the dinner for breakfast, where he informed me that we were going to spend the day at Opry Land. "Yay," I said, "you've thought of everything."

"I tried to," he said, "How do you feel about going out to some of the clubs tonight?"

"Sounds good, I love hearing all the great music, and always wonder why none of them are signed with a record company yet."

"Yeah, I know, but that's just how the business works."

"Yeah, tough break for them."

"I think you probably understand that more than I do."

"What do you mean?"

"Your writing."

"Oh, well I've decided that I'm not going to try to get it published. I just want to work at a publishing company. I want to help other writers get published."

"I thought it was your dream to get published?"

"Not exactly, I love writing, but it's so personal. I don't really want a ton of people reading it, just the people who are close to me."

"Okay, so go do the great deed of helping other writers. You'll do great."

"Thanks, so you still want to be a doctor, or are you thinking that's too long to be in school?"

"No, I want to be a doctor, even if school kills me. I'm going to get that damn degree."

"I'm proud of you."

"It's all thanks to you. If you hadn't gotten me to straighten my ass up junior year and actually do the work, I'd either still be in high school or be a high school drop out."

"No you wouldn't. Your parents would have never allowed that. Anyway you did all the work yourself; I just gave you a nudge."

"A nudge, more like a kick in the ass, you didn't pull in punches with me."

"True, I was a big time bitch."

"Yeah," he said and laughed at the shocked look on my face, "but that's what I needed. So thank you."

"Well your welcome. I'm always happy to give you a kick in the ass," I said with a gleam in my eye.

"Can it wait till later, I'd like to able to walk around Opry Land," he said grinning.

"Sure," I replied laughing.

Opry Land was great. I couldn't ride any of the rides because of my epilepsy, but I loved just walking around and looking in the shops. We spent all day there.

We went to a couple of different clubs that night, and heard a lot of great music. I was a little disappointed when Andy noticed I was getting tired. "Come on, time to get you to bed," he said getting up from our table.

"But there's another act coming on in a few minutes."

"Yeah, but you need sleep."

"Damn, okay, but all the good music."

"Will be here another time."

"Okay," I said. I fell asleep almost as soon as I sat down in the truck. I woke up when he sat me down on the bed. "Go back to sleep, sleeping beauty," he said giving me as kiss on the forehead.

"Okay," I said and was out again.

The next morning we got up, packed, checked out of the hotel, ate at the dinner on last time, and headed home. It had been a great weekend, one I would never forget.

Chapter Twelve

August 4, 2008

The day after my birthday someone unexpected showed up on my doorstep, someone not altogether welcome.

I was in the bed when I heard the knock on my front door. I got up wondering who the hell would be at my door at midnight. When I opened the door I was shocked and pissed. "What the hell are you doing here? You haven't talked to me in over a year, and all of sudden you show up on my doorstep. You can go to hell for all I care," I said. But as I started to shut the door I heard Jace say, "Jenni's dead."

I took a good look at him then. He looked awful. "Come in," I said on a sigh. He came in and collapsed on the couch. "Can I get you anything?"

"Do you have any whiskey? Never mind I don't need any more whiskey. I've stayed drunk for the past week."

"Okay, what happened, Jace?" I asked sitting down beside him.

"We had an argument. Jenni always goes for a walk when we argue. She walks off the mad. It was late. The guy didn't even see her. She was run over," Jace said as he started to cry.

"Oh my god, Jace, I'm so sorry," I said pulling him into a hug. After a few minutes he pulled away, and said, "I should go. I shouldn't have come here. It's not fair to you. You're right. I was wrong. I haven't talked to you in over a year. I'll go. I'm sorry." I grabbed his arm as he started to get up.

"No you don't. You're going to stay your ass right here. You don't need to be driving."

"Lily," he said shaking his head.

"No, you're staying and that's the end of it. Give me your keys," I said holding out my hand. He just looked at me. "If you don't I'll start searching you."

"Okay," he said pulling his keys out of his pocket, "here ya go."

"Okay, I'll go get you a blanket and a pillow. You can sleep on the couch." We both remembered a time when I wouldn't have hesitated to let him sleep in the bed with me, with no worries of him trying anything. But things change and even though he was hurting, I was still hurt by what he had done.

The next morning when I got up Jace was sitting in the kitchen staring off into space with a cup of coffee sitting on the table in front of him. "Hey," I said walking over to give him a hug. He jumped at the sound of my voice.

"Hey, I made coffee," he said in a dead voice. He looked awful.

"Did you sleep last night?"

"Not really, I just couldn't."

"Do you want to talk about it?"

"I don't know."

"Well what was the argument about?" I asked thinking it would help him to talk about it.

The argument played through his head. "What the hell is this?" Jenni asked holding a shoe box.

"What the hell Jenni? Why are you going through my stuff?" Jace retorted.

"No you don't. Answer the question Jace? Because it looks like letters to Lily."

"Jenni, it's not important."

"It's not important! There are a ton of letters in here. A ton of hidden letters. Why?"

"I miss her sometimes Jenni, that's all."

"That's all. I thought you said it was over, Jace. I thought you said you were over her."

"I am, but she was my best friend for years."

"Yeah, and you just see her as friend. Go to hell!" she yelled storming out the front door.

Jace looked up at me and said, "Nothing important. I think I'll go take a shower." Then he got up and left the room.

When I heard the shower come on, I picked up the phone and called Jane. "Hello," Jane said when she answered.

"Hey," I said having to pause before I could start the conversation. "Jace showed up on my doorstep last night."

"I'm not surprised. He told you about Jenni?"

"Yeah."

"I figured he'd eventually come to you. I doubt he'll be able to talk to anyone else."

"Do you know what happened?"

"A little bit of it."

"Do you know what they argued about?"

"No, he won't tell anyone."

"Yeah, I just asked him. He looked so haunted when I did. I thought he would tell me. All he said was nothin' and went to take a shower."

"Did he tell you when she died?"

"No."

"A month ago, he's stayed drunk for a month. He lost his job and his apartment. Lily you have to help him, please."

"I'll do my best, but I don't know if I can get through to him."

"I know you can. You've always been able to."

"But this is different. Someone he loved died, and I can tell he blames himself."

"Yeah, he does, but if anyone can get through to him, it's you. He won't listen to anyone else. We've all tried. Josh even tried. For once Josh isn't being an ass hole."

"How well did Jace take that?"

"Surprisingly he didn't even try to hit him. He just walked off."

"Well that's something."

"I think I would have preferred if he had hit him. Then I would have known Jace was still in there. It's like he's dead inside."

"Yeah, I know what you mean. He can stay with me as long as he needs. I'll do what I can Jane, but why didn't someone call me?"

"We didn't know if that was a good idea. We didn't know if Jace could handle seeing you, or if you would even want to be there for him."

"Of course I want to be here for him. He might have hurt me, but he's still my Jace."

"You haven't called him that since y'all were little."

"I know, but he still is. Well I've got to go. He's getting out of the shower. Bye girl."

"Bye."

When he came back in the kitchen he gave me a weird look, and asked "Isn't it Tuesday?"

"Yeah, why?"

"Don't you have class? I don't want you skipping just because I'm here."

"I'm not. I don't have any classes today."

"Okay," was all he said as he turned toward the living room.

I didn't ask any more questions the rest of the day. I could tell he wasn't ready to talk. At noon I left for work, "You sure you don't want to come with me? Trust me my boss won't mind."

"Naw, I'll just stay here."

"Okay, see you a little after nine. There's plenty of food in the kitchen, just fix you something if you get hungry."

"Okay, Lily go, I'll be fine."

"Okay, call me if you need anything."

"Kay." With that I left wondering if I should have just called in. I didn't know if it was a good idea to leave him alone.

August 8, 2008

Friday night, Jace and I had fallen asleep on the couch watching TV. I woke up when I heard the front door open. I looked up to see Andy standing in the door way. "What the hell Lily?" he said looking pissed. That woke Jace up. "Umm, I think I'll leave," Jace said getting up.

"No, you won't. You just stay here," I said looking at Jace. I turned to Andy and said, "You follow me." He looked like he wanted to argue, but he followed me into the bedroom.

"Lily, what the hell is he doing here? Have you forgotten he blew you off and hasn't spoken to you for over a year?"

"No, I haven't, but he's hurting Andy. I can't turn him away."

"He's hurting. What did he finally realize what a big mistake he made?" Andy asked sarcastically.

"Jenni died."

"What?"

"She was run over one night when she went for a walk. They had just had an argument."

"Well, I feel sorry for him, but that still doesn't give him a right to show up at your place. Lily, he treated you like shit. He was supposed to be your best friend and he pretty much told you to go to hell for no reason."

"Andy, he needs me. He was there for me when I needed someone. I can't just tell him to leave."

"Damn it Lily, why do you have to be so caring?"

"It's just who I am."

"If you help him, and he hurts you again I'm going to kick his worthless ass."

"Don't call him worthless, Andy. No one is worthless. I get you don't like him because of what he did, but he had his reasons."

"So all is forgiven just like that, Lily."

"No not just like that. I've been working on forgiving him for over a year, and Monday night when he showed up on my doorstep I finally managed it."

"Okay, why?"

"Because he came to me, Andy, he came to me. He came to me because he needed a friend. That let me know that we're still friends, let me know he still needs me."

"Well what about what you need?"

"Andy, I need him in my life. He's my best friend."

"Okay, whatever. I'm goin' home. I'll call you tomorrow."

"Andy, wait!" I yelled as he headed out of the bedroom.

"No, I don't want to talk to you right now," he said and walked out of the apartment.

I stood there shocked until Jace came up to me and gave me a hug. "I'm sorry. I didn't mean to cause problems between you and Andy," he said sadly.

"It's okay. It's not your fault."

"Lily, I heard everything y'all said. It wasn't like y'all were tryin' to be quiet," he said sheepishly when I gave him a hard look.

"It's still not your fault. Don't worry we'll patch it up. It's not like this is the first time we've had an argument about you. I guess I just thought he was over all of that."

"I think he was until I screwed up, and treated you like shit."

"Well maybe, but he'll come around."

"Are you sure? Do you want me to leave?"

"No, you're staying here until you're back on your feet, okay? I'm tired, time for bed big boy," I said trying to pull off a smile.

"Okay, night Lily, I love you," he said as I headed toward my bedroom. I stopped in my tracks, shocked.

162

"What did you just say?"

"I said I love you as a friend. You know that."

"Oh yeah, sorry," I turned around and gave him a hug, "Night, I love you too." With that we both went to bed, me in the bed, and him on the couch.

Jace lay on the couch awake for a while after that. "What the hell I'm a doing? Jenni just died and I'm telling Lily I love her. That's wrong in so many ways. I'm causing problems between her and Andy. I should just go, but I can't. I need her."

I was woken at three thirty the next morning by my phone ringing. "Hello," I said groggily.

"Hey," I heard Andy say. He was drunk.

"Hey Andy, have you been drinking?"

"Just a little."

"Yeah, I bet."

"Lily, I'm sorry. I was a jackass. If you need to help Jace then help him, but don't expect me to be nice to him. I don't think I can do that."

"Andy, I'm sorry I didn't tell you he was here, but I wasn't sure how you would react, and I guess I just wanted to postpone an argument."

"Yeah well, next time tell me. You had plenty of opportunities. We talk every day, Lily."

"I know."

"Well, I guess I'll let you get some sleep. I just noticed what time it is."

"Okay."

"One question first."

"What?"

"He's not sleeping in the bed with you, is he?"

"No Andy, he's sleeping on the couch."

"Good, let me know when he leaves. I'll come see you then."

"Andy, you can come see me with him here."

"No, I don't think I can."

"Andy?"

"Bye, love you," he said and hung up before I could say anything else.

I lay there for an hour wondering what I was going to do. I couldn't kick Jace out, but I didn't even know if I could help him. Andy had pretty much broken up with me because Jace was staying at my place. I couldn't choose between them. My best friend and my boyfriend, I loved them both, I needed them both.

Chapter Thirteen

August 12, 2008

When I walked into the kitchen Jace was sitting at the table staring off, the same way I had found him every morning since that first morning. "Mornin'," I said walking to the coffee pot. At least he always made coffee.

"Hey."

"I'm getting you out of the house today. So go get dressed. I'll cook breakfast. We'll leave after I get ready."

"Where are we goin'?"

"You'll find out when we get there."

"Lily, I don't know. I think I'll just stay here."

"No, you won't."

"Lily."

"No arguing. You're coming with me and that's the end of it."

"Yes ma'am," he said sarcastically, but he got up and went to take a shower.

An hour later we were on the road. "Well seeing as I'm the one who's driving you might need to tell me where were going," he said looking over at me.

"Johnson Construction, the office is right off the highway."

"What? Why are we going there?"

"You have a job interview."

"What? Lily, if you're getting tired of supporting me you could have just kicked me out."

"It's not that. It cost no more to support both of us than it does to support me, well not much more."

"Then what is all this about?"

"You need to stop sitting around the apartment all day. You need a distraction, and a job's the perfect distraction. Plus hammering away at something might help a little too."

"Lily, come on. I can get a job on my own."

"Yeah you can, but you need a little nudge. I couldn't keep waiting for you to get one. I couldn't keep watching you sit around the apartment and waste away."

"Okay, I'll do this for you."

"Do this for yourself."

"I don't know if I can do that, but I can do it for you."

"Whatever, as long as you do it," I said frustrated. It didn't feel like was I getting through to him at all.

When we got there I sat in the truck and let him go in by himself. I knew I had to make him do something on his own. I could hold his hand only so much. If he didn't start doing stuff on his own soon, he never would.

About an hour later he came out, I couldn't tell anything from his face. He got in the truck and I asked, "So?"

"I got the job. I start tomorrow."

"Good."

"Yeah, I guess."

"Think of it this way at least you'll have money to buy liquor so you can drink yourself to death. Cause I'm not buying it for you."

"Yeah, but if I started doing that you would kick me out."

"Naw, I'd just kick your ass. You could still stay with me, but you'd stay black and blue."

"Okay, I'll work, and I won't turn back into a drunk."

"Good, you're startin' to see things my way."

"What choice do I have?"

"None, because if you got tired of it and left I would just hunt you down and bring you back, you need some tough love at the moment."

"You've always been great at dishing it out," he said miserably.

"Hey, you came to me, remember? You knew what you were getting when you did. You came because you knew you needed it."

"Yeah, yeah, but that doesn't mean I have to like it."

"I know. So when are you going to start talking about it? You haven't mentioned it since the night you showed up at my door."

"I can't yet," he said sadly.

"Okay, I'm here whenever you're ready," I said understanding.

When I got up at six the next morning Jace was heading out the door. "Off to work?" I asked from behind him. He turned around and grimaced, "Yeah, my roommate threatened to kick my ass if I didn't."

"Ha-ha, have a good day," I said, "I have a break between classes at noon, you want to meet up and have lunch."

"Sure, how about we just meet up here?"

"Sounds good, see ya then."

"See ya."

A little after noon I walked into the apartment. Jace was busy fixing lunch, "Hey, turkey fine with you?" he asked as I walked into the kitchen.

"Sounds perfect," I said as I went to wash my hands at the sink.

"So, how's work so far?" I asked sitting down at the table with him.

"Okay, construction work is pretty much the same everywhere."

"Yeah, I guess it is. I wouldn't really know seeing as I've never worked construction."

"Yeah, I believe that's a good thing. Seeing as you're the clumsiest person I know," he said smiling.

"I've missed that," I said smiling back at him.

"Missed what?"

"Your smile."

"Oh," he said and stopped smiling.

"And I should have kept my mouth shut. Anyway, what time do you get off?"

"About five."

"Well I'll already be at work. I'll have a dinner break around six, you want to come by the store and eat supper together?"

"Sure, I'll cook something up."

"Your cooking," I sighed, "I've missed that too. You're almost as good of a cook as me."

"Yeah, well it's the least I can do for you."

"Your right," I said laughing, "If you want to cook for me every day you will hear no objections."

"Let's not go that far."

We finished up eating and then headed off our separate ways, "Don't forget six o'clock," I said walking toward campus.

"I won't. Do you want a ride?"

"No I like the walk."

"Okay, bye sweetie," he said giving me a kiss on the cheek.

"Bye."

Around six o'clock I watched Jace walk in the store carrying a plastic bag. "Hey," I said when he made it to the counter. "So what did you make me?"

"Spaghetti."

"You didn't have time to do spaghetti, unless you used store bought sauce. Which you never do?"

"I didn't use store bought sauce. I was planning on cooking for you soon. I made some sauce the other day while you were at school."

"How is it that I didn't know that?"

"Because I washed the dishes before you came home, and hid the jars in the very back of the cupboard."

"Why didn't we have spaghetti that day?"

"Because you'd already laid out chicken."

"Okay, just let me go clock out. The tables outside fine with you?"

"Yep, see ya there."

I met him outside. The spaghetti was great as it always is. "So, how was the rest of your day?" I asked while we ate.

"Okay, work," he replied. "How about you?"

"Same as usual, school then off to work. Busy, busy."

"You'd be bored around here if you weren't."

"Why do you say that?"

"Because we're in the city, and you prefer country life. You've never been into goin' out to clubs, shopping, and all that other stuff, at least not all that into it. You get bored with it quick, but give you a fishing pole or just a creek to sit by and your happy."

"True," I said, "So, you want to talk about it?"

"Talk about what?"

"Jace don't play dumb with me. If you don't want to talk about it just say no, but don't act dumb."

"Okay, no I don't want to talk about."

"Okay, fair warning I'm goin' to ask you that every day until you talk to me."

"I wouldn't expect anything less from you. As long as I can say no until I'm ready to talk, we're good."

"Okay."

A little while later Jace packed up the remnants of supper and left for home and I went back to work.

August 22, 2008

It had been two weeks since the last time I had talked to Andy, so to say I was surprised when he called that night would be an understatement. "Hello."

"Hey, it's me," I heard Andy say.

"Hey, I thought you didn't want to talk to me?"

"I'm sorry Lily. I just can't understand why you would put yourself in the position to get hurt by him again."

"He needs me right now, Andy. I can't just turn him away."

"I know. You're not that kind of person. That's one of the many reasons I love you. It's just hard for me to stand by and watch you walk down a path that is just going to hurt you in the end."

"You don't know he's going to hurt me."

"He's hurt you twice now, Lily."

"Yeah, but caring for someone means giving them a chance even when they've run out of chances."

"You're a much better person than I am."

"No, I'm just more understanding in some areas."

"Which means you're a better person than I am."

"Not really, but if you want to believe that then I guess I'll have to let you."

"So, is he still staying there?"

"Yeah, he started a new construction job last Wednesday. I think it's doing him some good to get out."

"How long is he going to stay there?" he asked angrily.

"I don't know Andy until he doesn't need to anymore," I said exasperated.

"Okay, okay, I'm sorry. I shouldn't jump on you about it."

"No, you shouldn't."

"How about you come to Auburn this weekend?"

"One I can't drive in case you've forgotten."

"I'll come get you."

"Two, I have to work."

"Call in."

"I can't. I need the money."

"He isn't helping you pay bills?"

"Yes, but I still need the money. I don't have a trust fund like you," I snapped.

"I know that," Andy snapped back. "Are you always going to hold my family's money against me?"

"No, I don't hold it against you, I'm sorry. I just don't think you get what it's like to be a working student."

"Sorry, I guess I don't always think about it. I just miss you so much."

"Why don't you come here?"

"Lily, baby, I can't do that with him there."

"Why not?"

"Because unlike when you asked me not to go off on your father, I don't think I can make you any promises with Jace."

"Fine," I said, "I guess I'll see ya the next weekend I have off."

"When is that?"

"I don't know."

"Okay, I love you baby."

"I love you too."

"Bye."

"Bye."

Jace walked in right after I hung up. "So, I got the good popcorn this time," he said as he walked in the door then he saw my face. "What's wrong?"

"Nothing," I lied.

"Don't lie to me Lily. I know when you're lying."

"Andy."

"Did y'all have another argument?"

"Not exactly, it was more of a very calm disagreement."

"Alright, are you goin' to be okay?"

"Yeah, we're workin' it out, but it's going very slowly."

"Y'all will work it out. Y'all always do, plus he's a good guy."

"Yeah, he is. So what movies did you get?" I asked plastering a smile on my face.

Chapter Fourteen

September 5, 2008

I finally got a weekend off, and decided to go see Andy. He was picking me up around five that evening, but I still didn't want to leave Jace alone. He still hadn't talked anymore about what happened to Jenni. So, I called Josh. I could tell Jace had finally forgiven Josh for whatever had happened years ago. I thought he might talk to his brother since he wouldn't talk to me.

I was in the bedroom packing when I heard the knock at the door. I stood there for a second listening, hoping I hadn't made a mistake. Then I heard Jace say sadly, "Hey Josh, what are you doing here?"

"Lily called me. Is that okay?"

"Yeah, it is. It's good to see you." And with that I let out the breath I hadn't even realized I'd been holding.

"Come in," Jace said, "So, how long are you here for?"

181

"The weekend if that's okay with you?"

"Fine with me."

"So, Lily didn't tell you she called me?"

"Nope, she was probably afraid I would get mad."

"I wasn't exactly sure what kind of welcome I would get, either."

"I'm sorry I've been a jackass the past few years, but you really hurt me when you did..." Jace broke off looking toward the bedroom door.

"You still haven't told her?" Josh asked in a whisper.

"No, she doesn't need to know. Y'all are friends too. I don't want to mess that up," Jace whispered back.

"Okay, but I don't see what you have to be sorry for. It was all my fault. I'm the one who started it when I..."

"Yeah, but you're my brother, I should have been willing to forgive you a long time ago."

"I didn't exactly make it easy."

"I know."

"I don't see why you were so worried about messing up mine and Lily's friendship or have you forgotten she broke my nose a couple of years ago? I deserved it, but she hasn't talked to me that much since then."

"She hasn't?"

"Well not like she used to. I said some really mean shit to her, and plus I did something really awful to her best friend."

"Yeah, and her best friend dumped her right after that. I'm sure y'all have talked more over the past couple of years than me and her."

"Possibly, so are you ever going to explain that bit of stupidity to me?"

"Yeah, I will, but a little later. Okay?"

"Okay. Are you up to telling me what happened the night Jenni died?"

"Maybe… We'll need alcohol, though. I don't think I can get through that conversation sober."

"Okay, we'll head to the liquor store in a little while. When's Lily leaving?"

"Right now," Jace said when he heard the knock on the door. He went and let Andy in. "She's in the bedroom."

"Okay," was all Andy said, and then he headed toward the bedroom.

"So, you taking in Josh too?"

"No, smart ass, I called him to see if he could get Jace to talk about what happened."

"Do you really think that's going to work? The whole time I've known them they've been at each other's throats."

"They weren't always like that. They used to be really close, and from what I just over heard I think they might be ready to get back to that."

"Okay, but if you come home to two dead bodies it's your fault."

"They're not going to kill each other. Let's go," I said grabbing my bag.

"Y'all have fun," I said giving Josh and Jace each hug, "or at least patch things up. Y'all need each other."

"Yes ma'am," they said in unison.

"Have fun, and don't worry about us," Jace said.

"Bye Lily," Josh said as I headed toward the door.

"Bye y'all."

An hour later while I was on my way to Auburn with Andy, Jace and Josh sat at my kitchen table with a bottle of Jack

Daniel's sitting between them. "So, where do you want to start, Lily or Jenni?"

"Well, I guess with what happened last year. Why I dumped Lily."

"Okay, why did you?"

"Because I knew I could never have her the way I wanted, but I knew I could have Jenni that way. I just had to give up being friends with Lily. I thought that would be a lot easier than it actually was. It killed me to see her with Andy, it still does. I was wrong though, it hurt more not to see her or talk to her at all."

"I'm sorry. I'm sorry I screwed that up for you. I was so damn stupid. I wanted her, and you had her. So instead of doing what was right, I lied and told her you slept with Renee. I wish I could take that back, but I can't."

"Just one question, why did you keep being a jackass to me after she broke up with me?"

"Because she didn't come running to me, she just left. She didn't come to me to be consoled. I didn't get the chance I thought I would. I realized I never had a chance with her. She would always see me as a little brother. And that pissed me off because she didn't see you that way."

"I'm sorry. I didn't know you had feelings for her until you told her I slept with Renee. I should have seen it, you are my brother."

"Yeah, well you were a little blinded by love."

"So when did you finally let go of it?"

"Right after the camping trip, I realized I wasn't being a jerk because I loved her and couldn't have her. I was being a jerk because I was mad I lost. I didn't love her that way, and never had. That was a tough revelation."

"I bet."

"So tell me about the night Jenni died?" Jace took a huge breath and said, "It was all my fault."

"Why would you say that?"

"Because it is, I came home from work and Jenni was holding a shoe box full of letters I had written to Lily."

"Huh?"

"I wrote letters to Lily for the whole year that we didn't talk. I never sent them. I just hid them away in a shoe box. Jenni found them. We argued about it," Jace said with a haunted look on his face.

"Jace, that doesn't make her death your fault," Josh said earnestly.

"Yes it does. If she hadn't been with me she would have never found those letters, we would have never argued, she would have never gone for a walk to calm down, and she would have never been run over. She would still be alive if it wasn't for me."

"You can't know that. Remember when we were little and you explained fate to me. It was right after our dog died. I was upset because I thought it was my fault. I didn't put is collar on tight enough so he got off. You told me that it was his time. That even if I had put the collar on right, that fate would have still taken him. You can't know that Jenni would still be alive if she hadn't been with you. You forget fate always gets what it wants one way or another."

"But…" Jace said starting to cry. Josh got up, walked around the table, and pulled his brother into a hug, and cried with him, for him.

While Josh held Jace through the worst of his pain, Andy and I arrived in Auburn. "So, what do you have planned for this weekend?" I asked.

"I was thinking we could stay in."

"Sounds good to me." We pulled up at his apartment then.

"So, what did you plan on doing with me all weekend?" I asked grinning as we headed up to his apartment.

"Well, how about I show you," Andy said throwing me over his shoulder as we both laughed.

Around midnight we sat in his kitchen eating grilled cheese sandwiches. "I've missed you so much," Andy said all of a sudden.

"I've missed you too," I said leaning over and giving him a kiss.

"I really am sorry I've been a jerk about this whole Jace thing. I'm startin' to get used to it."

"I'm sorry it's been so hard on you. I never meant to upset you. I just want to help Jace."

"I get it. I guess I would do the same thing if I was in your shoes, or at least I hope I'm a good enough person to at least try."

"You are, and I know you're just worried I'll get hurt again."

"I am, but it's your choice to make, not mine. And I haven't been making it easy on you."

"Well, I think we're making progress."

"Yeah, I do to. How about I come down next weekend?"

"That sounds great," I said smiling, glad we had finally worked it out.

Sunday evening Andy and I arrived back at my place just as Josh was leaving. Andy sat in the truck as I walked over to Josh's '97 Chevrolet Z71, "So, how did it go?" I asked.

"Good, thank you. Me and him are good again. And I think he might just be on the mend."

"Did he tell you what happened?"

"Yeah, but I'm not going to tell you," he said seeing the look on my face. "He'll tell you if he wants you to know. Do me favor?"

"Sure, what?"

"Don't ask him about it. Please Lily, don't. I think he's going to be able to handle it better now, but until he wants to tell you don't put him through it. I've never seen my brother that torn to pieces."

"Okay, I won't ask."

"Thanks," Josh said giving me a sad smile, "you're a great friend Lily James. I love you. Take care of my brother."

"I will. Love you too Josh." I headed into my apartment as Josh pulled off. I was happy him and Jace had worked everything out, but I wished someone would tell me what had happened the night Jenni died.

Andy met me at the door, "So?" he asked when he was beside me.

"It seems things went well, but I still don't know what happened the night Jenni died. Josh wouldn't tell me and he asked me no to ask Jace."

"You told him you wouldn't?"

"I promised I wouldn't, and I still don't know what the hell happened between Jace and Josh to begin with. Neither one of them has ever been forthcoming about it with me. Trust me I've asked a thousand times."

"Does anyone other than those two know?"

"Yeah, I think Jane and Nick do, but they won't tell me either."

"You think they do? Maybe they don't. Maybe they're just as confused as you are."

"They have an idea at least."

"Well maybe they don't want to tell you because they don't know if it's true or not."

"That's possible. You want to come in?"

"Naw, I got to get back. Sorry," he added at the look on my face.

"It's okay," I said, "drive safe. I love you." He bent down and kissed me, "I love you too. Now go take care of your friend. I'll call you later."

"Okay, bye."

"Bye."

Chapter Fifteen

October 4, 2008

"Are you sure you want to move out?" I asked Jace that morning while I helped him pack.

"Yes, and it's just next door," Jace said smiling, "I don't think you're going to miss me that much."

"Well, if you're determined."

"Lily, it's not like I'm moving to another country, it's just next door."

"I know. I've just gotten used to you being here."

"I know, but you can knock on my door anytime."

"Same goes."

"I know one person who's happy I'm moving."

"Andy?"

"Yep."

"He's over all of that now."

"Yeah, but I'm sure he'll be glad for y'all to have the place all to y'alls selves when he's down," Jace said wiggling his eyebrows and grinning.

"Shut up," I said hitting him then I grinned and said, "Well now that you mention it, can you move any faster?"

"Ha-ha, funny, you little wench."

"I love you too. Now hurry up and get out. Andy'll be here soon, and that time alone sounds really great," I said laughing as Jace rolled his eyes at me.

A few hours later we had Jace completely moved. Andy knocked on the door just as I was sitting down to relax. "Come in," I yelled, "I'm too tired to move."

"Hey," Andy said smiling as he came in. "Did he work you to death today?"

"Almost, you could've come earlier and helped," I said giving him a pointed look.

"Yeah, well I was busy," he said nowhere near convincingly.

"Yeah right, busy doing what?"

"Umm, nothin' actually, but I'm not very good at the moving so y'all were better off without my help."

"Bull shit, you helped me move in here. You just didn't want to help."

"True, are you going to hold it against me?"

"Maybe, maybe not."

"What do have to do to get that answer to become a no?"

"Massage," I said smiling.
"Okay," he said grinning.

"Not that kinda massage. I need a back massage and a foot massage. Get to work mister."

"Yes ma'am."

Josh also came down that weekend to spend some time with Jace. "So big brother, how does it feel to be out on your own again?" Josh asked.

"Good, I guess."

"You miss her already, don't you?"

"No, she's right next door."

"Yep, she is. She's right next door with Andy."

"So what? She's with Andy, has been for almost two years now."

"Yeah, I know, but you've been in love with her your whole life, and have yet to tell her. Are you ever going to tell her?"

"I don't know. I can't think about being with anyone right now."

"Okay, I can understand that, but what about in the future? Are you just goin' to stand back and watch Lily marry someone else?"

"What? Their getting married?" Jace asked panicking.

"Not that I know of, but if you don't say something soon she's going to end up marrying someone else."

"She's only nineteen; I doubt she's going to marry anyone anytime soon."

"Yeah, but at the pace you've been going you won't tell her how much you love her until you're on your death bed."

"Okay, okay, I get your point."

"Good, just think about. I'm not saying tell her today, or tomorrow, or even a month from now. When the time is right you'll know, just don't let the chance pass you by."

"Okay," Jace said, "By the way you're buying supper."

"What?"

"I'm broke. I had to pay a deposit and first's month's rent on this place today."

"Whatever, nothin' expensive."

"Okay, I was thinkin' a steak," Jace said grinning.

"Ha-ha, I'm thinkin' pizza," Josh retorted as Jace laughed.

October 6, 2008

Monday evening after I got out of class and Jace got off work we met up at our favorite diner for supper. "So, how was your weekend?" Jace asked wiggling his eyebrows after we'd ordered.

"Good, pervert, how about yours?"

"It was good. I'm glad me and Josh are getting along better now. I've missed my little brother; you know the one he was before he became a jackass."

"Yeah I know what you mean. I've missed that Josh too," I agreed. "So are y'all ever going to tell me what happened

199

between the two of you?" You Jace thought, but instead said, "Nothing important enough to keep us from being brothers for three years." Well, that's a lie he thought, but better than telling her the truth.

I could tell he was lying to me, but he'd been lying to me about this for years, why did it matter anymore. "So, I want to tell you a secret," I said.

"Okay, spill."

"I'm thinking about changing my major."

"Okay, to what?"

"Psychology."

"Well, that's good. If that's what you want then do it."

"You don't think I should stick with English. I mean I've always loved books, but..."

"But you're more interested in psychology now."

"Well not exactly. I want to be able to really help people."

"I should have known," Jace said smiling, "If that's what you want do it. You'll be great at it."

"I don't know. I didn't help you all that much."

"Yes you did."

"No, I didn't. Josh did."

"You got me and Josh together, big accomplishment, and if you hadn't taken me in I'd probably be dead."

"No you wouldn't."

"Yeah I would. I'd been contemplating suicide for a while, but you reminded me every day that I have something to live for. You let me know it would get better if I would just let it."

"I did?"

"Yeah, you did. You kept me sane. You pulled me out of my darkest period. Lily, you saved my life."

"But you never talked about it."

"I couldn't, and still can't, tell you all of it. Some of it involves you Lily, and that's all I'm going to say."

"What? No you can't do that. You can't tell me that and nothing else."

"Yeah, I can. I might tell you one day, but for now you're better off not knowing."

"Great, I need a therapy session now."

"What?" Jace said looking worried.

"Don't worry. I think that every now and then. I have for the past couple of years. When anything overwhelms me therapy jumps into my head. But I remember everything Dr. Johns told me and I get through it."

"I didn't know that. How did I not know that?"

"Because I didn't tell you, until now. Actually no one knows that, so don't tell please."

"I won't," Jace said as the waitress brought our food to the table.

October 31, 2008

Halloween, Andy and I had a party to go to. I decided to go as a vampire, actually a specific vampire, Zoey from the House of Night books. Andy was going as Captain Jack Sparrow. "A vampire and a pirate, interesting," Jace said.

"Why? What's wrong with it?" I asked.

"Nothing, I'm just surprised y'all aren't doing the whole matching costumes deal."

"You know I don't do the whole matching thing. I can't stand that crap."

"Yeah, but I figure Andy would talk you into it."

"Please not even he could talk me into that."

"So what time is he supposed to pick you up?"

"Six."

"You better hurry its five thirty and you're running around in your underwear."

"Damn it, help me into my costume." He picked it up off the bed and said, "Where's the rest of it?"

"Ha-ha, very funny," I said snatching it out of his hand, "Just zip me up."

"Okay, but you know you could catch pneumonia going out in nothing but that, its freezing out there."

"It's not that cold. Plus I'll be wearing a coat while I'm outside."

"Okay, well I guess I'm going to go before the guy with the sword shows up."

"Okay, see ya later."

"Bye."

Thirty minutes later Andy walked into the bedroom as I was finishing up my make-up. "Well damn, I should have taken you to a costume party before now," he said grinning.

"Why? You've seen me in less."

"True, but I know I'm going to be with the hottest girl in the room. Every other guy is going to be jealous."

"Whatever," I said rolling my eyes. "I've got something I want to tell you."

"Okay, what?" Andy asked looking worried.

"I changed my major this morning."

"To what?" he asked, his eyebrows lifting, not a good sign.

"Psychology."

"Why?"

"Because I want to do something to help people, why are you getting mad?"

"I don't know. I guess I'm just surprised. This is the first time I've heard you mention."

"Sorry, I just wanted to make my mind up first."

"It's okay. So psychology?"

"Yeah, I've been thinking about ever since Jace showed up."

"Oh, well that's great," he said in a weird tone.

"What's wrong?"

"Nothing, you ready?"

"Yeah," I said looking at him quizzically.

"Good, let's go. I don't want to be late."

"Okay."

Chapter Sixteen

November 22, 2008

Josh and Renee showed up on my doorstep, together.

"Hey guys," I said when I answered the door, "come on in."

"Hey, is Jace at home?" Josh asked.

"I think he is. Why don't you go knock and see?"

"Yeah, okay," Josh said and headed back out.

"Can I use your bathroom?" Renee asked.

"Yeah, it's right through there."

"Thanks."

"Okay, what the hell is goin' on?" I asked Andy.

"I don't know. She's your sister, and he's Jace's brother," Andy answered.

"It doesn't make any sense for them to come together. They've never gotten along."

"Well, I guess we're about to find out," Andy said as Josh and Jace walked in the front door, and Renee came out of the bathroom.

Jace looked at me quizzically, and I shrugged in answer. "Well, y'all must be wondering' why we're here," Renee said.

"Yeah," I answered.

"Well, we got married," Josh said.

"What?" Jace and I said in unison.

"What the hell Renee?" I yelled just as Jace looked at Josh and yelled, "What the hell were you thinking; y'all don't even like each other."

"Well, I think I'm going to leave," I head Andy whisper as he headed for the door.

"Okay, okay, calm down," Renee yelled. "Look I know Josh and I didn't get along growing up, but we've actually been together for about a year."

"Wait why are we just hearing about this?" I asked.

"Well, at first you and Jace weren't talking, and we didn't want to make either one of you uncomfortable. And well Jace and Josh weren't talking either. And then Jace lost Jenni. There never seemed to be a good time."

"Okay, so who all knows you're married?" Jace asked looking exhausted all of a sudden.

"Just y'all, we wanted y'all to be the first to know," Josh said sheepishly.

"Well, congratulations," I said. Jace gave me a confused look and I just shrugged.

"Yeah, congratulations," Jace repeated.

"See I told you they wouldn't take it too bad," Renee said looking at Josh.

"Yeah," Josh said knowing exactly what Jace and I were thinking. How long is this going to last?

They left not long after that to go inform the rest of their families. "So, Josh and Renee," I said after they had left.

"Yeah, what the hell are they thinking?" Jace asked.

"I don't know, but of course neither one of us knew they were dating each other either."

"Yeah how did we miss that one?"

"I never saw the two of them together, and you pretty much never saw your brother."

"Okay, should we give them the benefit of the doubt?"

"Yeah, I think so. I mean they've been together a year, so who knows it might work."

"Do you think she's pregnant?"

"Renee wouldn't get married just because she's pregnant. She can be stupid, but not that stupid."

"Okay, good to know. She's four years older than him," Jace said starting to laugh.

"Are you actually finding this funny or are you laughing to keep from crying?"

"It is funny. Think about it, if you had asked anybody in our families to pick the two who would run off and get hitched they would have said me and you, Josh and Renee would never have entered into their minds," he said as I started to laugh too.

"Okay, you're right. It's funny in an ironic way."

"Oh just think about our families' reaction," he said and we both collapsed laughing.

"Oh, I almost wish I could be there," I said holding the stitch in my side.

"Yeah, as a fly on the wall, if anyone actually saw us they'd jump on us about it. 'Why did you let them do this? It was supposed to be you two.' I think I'd rather have the second hand account," Jace replied.

"True," I said, "want a drink?"

"Do you have alcohol?"

"Of course," I said walking to the kitchen to get the bottle of Jack.

"How is it you always have alcohol? You're only nineteen and so is your boyfriend."

"I have my connections. What about you? You're only nineteen, and you usually have alcohol."

"Okay, good point. We have the same connection, don't we?"

"Of course, the same one we've had since we were sixteen."

"Should've known he didn't just do it for me. He's always liked you more anyway."

"Yeah, I know," I said pouring us each a glass, "Lets see I guess we should drink to Renee and Josh."

"Yeah, to Renee and Josh, may they not kill each other."

Around seven that evening Andy showed back up,

"Hey," he said walking in the door. "Are y'all drunk?" He asked

looking at the half empty bottle of Jack on the coffee table.

"Just a little," I answered smiling.

"Just a little, huh. Yeah I'd say more than a little."

"Naw, this isn't really drunk. You should have seen us the night

Lily broke up with me," Jace said.

"Hey now, we swore we would never talk about that," I said

slurring.

"Oops, sorry my tongue gets a little loose when I'm drunk."

"True, so what secrets can I get out of you?" I asked seeing an

opportunity through the drunken haze. Unfortunately those

were the exact words to sober Jace up, "Nothin', I'm goin' to

head home. See y'all later," he said rushing toward the door.

"Damn, I thought I would finally find out what that damn

argument was about?"

"Which one?" Andy asked sitting down on the couch beside me.

"All of them, any of them," I replied. "I think I'm sobering up. That might be a good thing. What time is it anyway?"

"Seven."

"That would explain why you were so shocked to see us drunk."

"Yep, so how long have y'all been at it?"

"Since Renee and Josh left."

"They threw y'all for a loop."

"Yeah, it's just strange. They've never really like each other, and when Jace and I were together they stayed at each other's throat. I guess that's the last time I saw them hang around each other."

"Well, stranger things have happened. Do you really think they won't make it?"

"I don't know. This is the first I've even heard about them being a couple, they might actually be good together."

"So we're giving them the benefit of the doubt."

"Yep, I just needed a few drinks first."

"Yeah, I can see that, and it seems Jace needed them too."

"Yeah, he's probably drinking a huge pot of coffee right now. He was never really much for drinking, or at least getting drunk. He hasn't been drunk since the weekend Josh came down, before he moved out."

"Yeah, I remember that weekend, for completely different reasons," Andy said leaning over to give me kiss. "So would you like a distraction from all of the family drama?"

"I'd love one," I said grinning, "Why don't you unplug the phone?"

"Good idea. Your phone will probably start ringing here soon."

"Yep, I don't want to hear about it until tomorrow."

"Sounds like we're going to have a busy night."

"Oh I hope so."

While Andy and I were *busy*, Jace was busy getting drunk. It seems I was a little wrong about how well he was doing, a lot wrong. He sat at his kitchen table with a bottle of Jack staring at a picture. A picture of Jenni he carried around with him at all times. What I didn't know, what no one knew, was that since he got a job and moved out he'd been getting drunk every night. He would sit alone in his apartment, look at the well worn picture of Jenni, and drink until he passed out. "I'm sorry Jenni. You deserved better," he whispered to the face in the picture. Then he grabbed the bottle and headed to his bedroom. He passed out an hour later, with tears still wet on his cheeks.

Chapter Seventeen

January 2, 2009

I was packing for mine and Andy's trip to Tennessee, when Jace walked in. "So, where are the happy couple headed off to this weekend?"

"Nashville. It's kinda become our place I guess. He took me last year for our anniversary."

"Cool, hope y'all have fun."

"We will, we always do."

"Good, so what do you need me to do while you're gone?"

"Nothing really, umm, check my mail tomorrow. I don't have any real plants because I always kill them, and no pets because of the landlord. So, I guess you get off easy."

"Yep."

"What are you doin' this weekend?"

"Going out with some of my buddies from work," he lied without missing a beat.

"You've been doing that a lot here lately. I'm glad. You need more friends than just me. You need some guys to hang out with."

"Oh come on, you know you'll always be one of the guys," Jace said jokingly.

"Yeah, do you know how many years I hated that? I'm over it now, but damn it sucked for a while there."

"Did it? Let me guess about the time you started being interested in boys as more than punching bags?"

"Yeah."

"I'm going to tell you a secret. You can't tell anyone."

"Okay."

"We all stopped seeing you as one of the guys about that time, we were just too afraid to do anything about it."

"You're just saying that."

"Nope, god's truth."

"Really, hmm, wish I'd known that then. I would have loved making y'all drool."

"You did that anyway, we just did our best to hide it."

"Hmm, that's an image that is going to stay with me. I like it," I said grinning.

"Good, now go have fun. I think I just heard Andy pull up."

"Okay, see ya later. Love ya," I said giving him a hug and kiss on the cheek.

"Yeah, you too, bye Lily," he said following me out the door.

Andy and I headed out then. "So, you ready to have some fun?"

"Of course, I love our trips to Nashville."

"Me too," Andy said. He looked a little nervous, but I just shrugged it off. I figured it was just school, and I knew he'd want to forget about school and everything else for the weekend. We'd talk about it when we got back. It was time for nothing but fun.

As Andy and I pulled out Jace went into his apartment, grabbed a bottle of Jack, and started drinking himself into a stupor.

The weekend was great, just what we needed. We both had a great time, but of course great things don't last. At midnight Monday morning, Andy looked over at me in bed and said, "I have something to ask you."

"Okay, ask away," I said having no clue what was coming. He got out of bed and went to get something out of his suitcase. He came back and sat down on the bed and opened it. It was a beautiful engagement ring. I was shock into silence. "Lily, I love you with all my heart. Will you marry me?"

At those words an image flashed into my head, not of Andy proposing though, but of Jace proposing and me saying yes. I looked at Andy with tears in my eyes. I knew I couldn't marry him. I loved him, but not the way he deserved. In that moment I realized that I'd always been in love with Jace, and that that would never change. "Andy, I'm so sorry," I said as tears ran down my cheeks, "I love you, but not the way you deserve. I can't marry you."Andy stared at me shocked for a few seconds then he got up, got dressed, and left.

I waited an hour before I started calling him. I called him ten times and he never picked up. After the tenth phone call I got a text, stop calling was all it said. So I stopped calling him. I sat there for a minute wondering what to do then I called Jace. "Come on Jace pick up, please," I whispered into the phone, but he didn't. I called him fifteen times before I gave up.

I sat there and cried for an hour then I tried one more person. "Hello," Jane said sleepily.

"Hey, I'm sorry I called so late, but I need some help."

"Lily? What's wrong? You sound like you're crying."

"Not at the moment. I'm in Nashville, and I need to come home."

"Okay, where's Andy? Isn't it y'alls anniversary weekend?"

"Yeah, umm, we broke up. So I really need to come home."

"Okay, we'll be there as soon as possible. Sweetie it's going to be okay. I promise." I hung up the phone and started to pack.

Andy hadn't returned to the hotel room when I left around six thirty that morning. I left him a note, apologizing again, even though I knew it wouldn't help, and telling him that Nick and Jane were coming to get me, just in case he worried when he got back and I was gone. Then I went to the diner down the street to wait on Nick and Jane.

At seven I saw them pull into the parking lot. I ran out to meet them. "Oh sweetie, what happened?" Nick asked giving me a hug.

"I...I don't know if I can talk about it yet."

"Okay, then we won't push," Jane said giving Nick a pointed look. "Lets get you home."

"Thanks, umm, have y'all heard from Jace?"

"No, why?" Nick answered.

"I tried to call him last night and he never answered. It's probably nothing. He was probably just out having fun."

"Yeah, I'm sure that's all it is," Jane said looking worried.

We arrived at my apartment around one that evening. I took my stuff in, and decided to go check on Jace. He wasn't in the living room; he wasn't in the kitchen. I found him in his bedroom passed out on the bed. He had a liquor bottle in one hand, and a picture in the other, a picture of Jenni. "Oh my god," I whispered and started trying to wake him up. He woke up long enough to give me a hard look and then was out again.

I went to work then. I started getting rid of all the alcohol in the house. I found more than I thought I would, plus a lot of empties.

I didn't sleep that night. I just sat there beside him on the bed staring at him. "Oh sweetie, how did I not know?" I whispered running my fingers through his hair. He woke up around one the next morning. He reached over to the night stand, looking for a bottle, it wasn't there. "Hey," I said from the other side of the bed. He looked over at me surprised. "Aren't you supposed to be in Nashville?"

"Yeah, didn't work out like I'd planned. Looking for something?"

"Umm, no. Why?"

"I figured you might be looking for the bottle of Jack that was sitting there when I came in."

"Huh, what are you talking about?"

"Don't play dumb with me, Jace. I'm not in the mood for it. Why didn't you tell me?"

"I'm fine. Just partied a little too much this weekend."

"I doubt all the booze in the house was from this weekend, and partying doesn't usually involve passing out with a bottle in one hand and a picture in another."

"Lily... I..."

"I know, okay, I know. I'm going to help you. Not too long ago I came to you when I needed help, and you got me help. I should have done the same for you in the beginning. I just thought I could help you myself. I was wrong, but I'm going to truly help you now. When the mental health clinic opens we will be there."

"What if I say no?"

"I'm not leaving you alone until you go and get help."

"You'll have to leave eventually."

"No, I won't. So are you going to do this the easy way or drag it out?"

"I'll go. Lily I'm sorry," Jace said looking pitiful.

"I'm sorry, Jace. I should have paid better attention."

"No, it's not your fault. Remember not too long ago I told you I should have seen what was going on with you."

"Yeah."

"And what did you tell me?"

"I hid it, so you wouldn't see, and I'm good at hiding when I want to."

"Exactly, and this time it was me hiding. It's just everything was going so well for you, I didn't want to mess that up for you."

"You could never mess anything up for me, Jace. You make my life better. You always have. You're my best friend."

"Have you gotten any sleep? You look like crap."

"Not really."

"Well, lay down. We'll both get some sleep. I think we're going to need it."

"Okay," I said laying down and curling into him.

At seven the alarm clock went off, we got up, got dressed, and headed to the clinic. "Do you want me to go in with you?" I asked Jace when we got there.

"No, I need to do this myself. Will you wait for me in the waiting room though? It'll be good to see you when I come out."

"Of course," I agreed giving him a hug, "I'm proud of you."

"Why?"

"For taking the first and hardest step, getting help."

"Thank you, for giving me the push I needed."

"Okay, let's go. If we don't go in, you won't get that help." We went in and surprisingly they took Jace back not long after he signed in. I sat in the waiting room worrying about him, worrying about Andy, and lastly myself. He came out an hour later, he looked exhausted. It was a start. I got up walked over to him, gave him a hug, and said, "I'm proud of you. I love you. You can get through this."

"Thanks, I love you too."

"Let's go. I'll fix you some breakfast and call your boss and tell him you're sick."

"Okay, let's go."

Chapter Eighteen

May 28, 2011

I had finally graduated from college, and I'd finally got my license back. My life was going pretty well. Jace was a lot better. He no longer blamed himself for Jenni's death. He still hadn't told me what all had happened that night, but I found that it didn't matter so much to me anymore. What mattered was that he was fine now. He was even thinking about starting his own construction company. I was starting my new job in less than a month. I was to be a therapist at the clinic that helped Jace. We were still best friends, still neighbors.

We were back in Jackson's Gap for the weekend. My family and friends were throwing a graduation party for me. I was in town picking up some stuff for the party when I ran into Andy. "Hey," I said standing in the drink aisle when I saw him.

"Hey," he said smiling and giving me a hug. I was surprised, he actually seemed happy to see me.

"So, how have you been?" I asked.

"Good, I just got married a few months ago."

"Wow, congratulations," I said happy for him.

"How about you?"

"I graduated. I have a job at the mental health clinic in Troy. I start in about a month."

"That's great. How's Jace?"

"He's good."

"Good to hear. So when are the two of you getting married?"

"Huh, where would you get an idea like that?"

"Because you two love each more than humanly possible."

"We're just friends."

"What? I figured you went back to Troy and y'all finally got together."

"No, I went back to Troy; found Jace in his apartment passed out. It turns out he wasn't doing as well as we all thought. I got him help, and was finally there for him like he needed."

"Oh."

"Yeah, well he's a lot better now. He's thinking about starting his own construction company."

"That's good. Well, I've got to go. The wife's waiting on me. It was good to see you," Andy said giving me another hug.

"You too."

I finished my shopping and headed back to Momma's. Jace met me at the door, "Need some help?" he asked holding the door open for me.

"Yep, there's plenty more in the car."

After we had gotten everything in the house we went outside to relax. "So, are you sure you want the party here?" he asked surprising me.

"Yeah, why wouldn't I?"

"Well, we usually have your celebrations at the creek. We all camp out and party."

"Yeah, but the city closed off the creek."

"Well we could find somewhere else to camp if you want."

"Nah, it wouldn't be the same. I think a house party with family and friends is perfect. Plus my mom wouldn't come camping, and I really want to celebrate this with her."

"Okay, whatever you want beautiful," he said grinning at me. "What?" he said seeing the look on my face.

"Oh, nothing, I just ran into Andy at the store."

"Talk about burying the lead."

"It wasn't that big of a deal."

"Yeah right, y'all broke up when he asked you to marry him and you said no. So of course running into him would be nothing," Jace said sarcastically rolling his eyes.

"He seemed happy. He's married."

"I know."

"How do you know?"

"I ran into him the last time I came up to see Josh."

"Oh, why didn't you tell me?"

"I didn't know how you would react. I didn't want to upset you."

"I'm not upset. I'm happy for him. I wasn't the one for him. I'm glad he found her."

"So, what put that look on your face then?"

"Oh nothing, he just said something weird that's all."

"What did he say?"

"Well, actually he asked me when we were going to get married, me and you."

"Oh well, I guess he never did get over me being your ex," Jace said, but thinking, well, there's my answer, just friends.

"Yeah, I guess."

April 18, 2012

I headed over to Jace's as soon as I got off work. I loved his new house. I couldn't believe he actually had a house. He did great job fixing it up. When I walked in I heard music. I walked back to the kitchen to find him cooking. "Hey, Brantley Gilbert?" I asked from behind him.

"Well, I figured I'd play something you like for once."

"You like his music too."

"Not as much as you. I swear you have the biggest crush on him."

"I like his music and his hot," I said laughing.

"Well, sit down dinner's almost ready."

"Good, I'm starving."

Jace sat the food on the table a minute later. As we sat there eating and joking around I looked at him and finally realized something I should have seen years before. "You didn't cheat on me," I said all of a sudden.

"What?" Jace looked up shocked.

"In high school when we were dating, you didn't cheat on me with Renee."

"No."

"But why would Josh lie? Why didn't you tell me the truth?"

"Josh had feelings for you. He thought if he could get me out of the way he could have you. I didn't tell you because you believed him. You trusted him and not me."

"I'm so sorry."

"What made you finally realize the truth?"

"I was just looking at you. Thinking of how far you've come. How far we've come since then. How you've been there for me, and everything else. And all of a sudden it made no sense. You cheating on me made no sense."

"Well, I'm happy to hear it."

"Jace, if I had realized this years ago we wouldn't have gone through so much pain. If I had realized this years ago we would probably be married by now."

"Yeah, but I don't think I would change the past. We are who we are because of it."

"And the people we are, are they destined to be just friends, or can I finally follow my heart."

"Oh thank god," Jace said coming around the table. "Do you know how long I've waited for you to say that?"

"I love you."

"I love you too." In the background I could hear "Fall into Me"

playing. To this day it is my favorite song.